One Saved to the Sea

by Catt Kingsgrave

Circlet Press, Inc.
Cambridge, MA

One Saved to the Sea

The oar sliced the air with a whirring noise, and clipped the side of Durn Helzie's skull neatly. Not a killing blow, but it was enough to spin the man like a top and sling the gray pelt from his fingers as he measured his length on the mossy stones of the holm. Mairead put herself between him and his prize, kicking the skin well behind her just to be sure.

Around the seaward edge of the holm, seals were diving from every stone, speckled gray and honking in alarm at the sudden intrusion in their basking night. In only a few seconds, the tiny islet was empty of all but herself and Helzie, who was curled up tight as a limpet, clutching his head and cursing her soundly.

"You mind your tongue, Durn Helzie," she snarled at him in the very voice that had always reminded his sort at school that she'd three older brothers and a very protective Da waiting on her displeasure. "You've no business out here but for thieving, and we both know it!"

"You cow, you bloody cow!" he spat, making as if to rise until she brandished the oar again. "This were no business of yours—"

"And isn't it my business when you come poaching on Meur lands then?"

"Poaching!"

"Aye," she said, choking short her grip on the oar so she could stoop to catch up the sealskin one-handed. "There's other names for it too, but as I'm a lady, I'll refrain."

"You, a lady?" He spat and grimaced. "It's you're a—"

"It's I'm well prepared to soften that skull of yours again if you come at me, and I'll thank you to remember that," she called over the crash as the sea battered the holm, filling the air with salt spray and the promise of a turning tide. "You're drunk, you're poaching, and you're trespassing. I won't have you insulting me into the bargain. Now up you get. Back to the trink and off our land before the tide comes in, or see if my Da and his gun don't have something to say about it."

He snickered, then yelped as she sliced the air just above his head, so close the oar snagged in his fair curls. "Augh, you're as mad as he is, you wretched cow!"

"Furious," she agreed. "Now march!"

He did stand, and carefully, holding one hand against his head while the other crept toward the pocket of his mac. Mairead hefted the oar again, and he thought better of it, though bitterly. "Aye, I'll go," he said, "but not without what's rightful mine."

Mairead shook her head, clutched oar and pelt tight in her fists. "You're taking away only what you brought, Helzie. Nothing else here belongs to you by any right."

"That skin's mine," he said, taking a single, wobbly step. "I won it square—"

"You wasn't born wearing it," Mairead replied, "and her that was will be wanting it back again." He took another step, teetered again, and clutched his head, but even in the moonlight Mairead did not miss that canny look in his eye. She was not surprised when he sprang at her, arms wide to tackle her down.

Her second swing at his head was not quite so polite as the first had been. This time when Helzie spun and dropped, he lay crumpled where he'd fallen, panting and moaning as the spite leaked out of him along with his ale. "Been robbed..." he mumbled against the lichens as his eyes rolled closed.

"That, I'll allow," she answered, "though you've had it coming for years." Then she turned and left him there.

The moon was full and high, fat and silver in a sky dark and clear of cloud—a rare night indeed in the Orkneys, which saw cloudless skies a bare handful of times in any given year. The moon offered light aplenty for Mairead to search the holm for the seal girl, and return her skin.

She knew which it had been—the freckled hide had one hind fin slightly ragged, as though torn in some fight, and one of the seal girls always danced with the ghost of a limp when they all came ashore on the holm. It was easy to pick her out among the whirl of flashing limbs by the way her moves did not quite match, and so it was she whom Mairead usually watched, hid in a crevice of rock above the steep path from the trink.

The moonlight revealed no soft curve of white skin on the river-mouth island; no trembling whorl of wood-dark hair in the shadows of sea-carved stone. Mairead quickly crossed the holm, peering into every crack of stone she could find, knowing there could never have been an extra skin among the seal folk, knowing that her limping girl must surely be hiding somewhere close by.

But soon she had to admit defeat. There were not many places to truly hide on the narrow spit of stone. The sea was relentless, and polished all it could not swallow down to smooth humps of rock where only weed and lichens could cling. Even the sandy beach on the lee side, where she dug cockles in the summer, was empty and white as a shell beneath the moon, marred only with the beached rowboat that must have brought Helzie down from the fisheries upstream. She climbed back to the top of the holm one last time, soft-footed as she could go, just in case the girl might have crept out of hiding while she'd been below.

And there she was, perched on the seaward edge of the holm, looking beautiful and forlorn with her dark hair carving waves down the soft curve of her shoulders. She made no sound, did not shiver or moan, but Mairead felt sure her lovely girl was weeping. And before she thought better of it, she found herself drawing the silky pelt from beneath her coat, and calling soft, "It's all right, I've got it right here—"

In a flash of white skin and dark, startled eyes, the selkie girl was gone, over the side and into the thrashing sea below without so much as a squeak of alarm. Mairead rushed to the edge, stared down the thrust of stone, twenty feet or more into the water, but the moonlight helped her pick out no human shape against the foam.

"Come back," Mairead called to the restless wind, knowing it useless. "You can have it back, I don't want it, I promise..."

She was disappointed to get no reply, but she couldn't say she was surprised.

"Ow, mind me head, woman!"

"Quit your bleating, or I'll make you ride in the back," Mairead grumbled, wrestling the old truck square on the coast road again. "You'd deserve it if I did."

Eager as she was to be rid of Helzie's company, there was only so fast she dared drive on the hilly, pitted track from the lighthouse promontory down to Ramphollow. The slant of the setting moon made shadows tricksy things, and her father's old truck could only handle so much punishment. Breaking an axle out here would only prolong the torment. The dinghy in the back scraped and bashed about the bed with its oars, but made less aggravating noise than her passenger.

"And now you'd crush me to death under a boat as well?" He shook his head, and shot her a snide look from under the plaster on his brow. "It's a cold welcome you are, Mairead Meur, and no mistake. Small wonder no man on the island will have you."

I have every man I want, she thought angrily, swerving to hit a rut square on and jounce the man into the ceiling again, *and that's none of them!* But aloud, she offered only, "It's a piece of luck for me that all the men on the island worth having have gone off to do their rightful duty then, isn't it, Durn Helzie?"

"Here then," he said, voice taking on the wheedling tone of excuses not even he believed, "Me asthma's—"

"Your asthma didn't stop you sneaking out to the holm and raiding my lobster pots in a stolen boat by moonlight, I notice," she said, gearing down to take the rising ground. Ahead, the Freystane split the moon disk like a knife thrust up from the hill crest. Not far now, thank God.

"Lobster pots!"

"Aye, seeing as how you'd no other business out on our land in the dark of night."

"I had!" he spat, going red in the dashboard glow as the great standing stone's shadow painted the road black around them. "I had and you know it, you cow! You'd no right to interfere, and I'll see you pay—"

She stomped the brakes, setting the truck's back end wobbling about madly on the gravel. Durn's threats evaporated into a wheezing screech, and he grabbed the dash in both hands as they slid to a stop at the crest of the hill. The truck's headlamps blazed square at lichen-stained granite from an arm's length away, until dust billowed up to soften the glare.

"Get out," Mairead said in the ringing, dust settling, metal pinging silence that followed. "Get out of my truck, Durn Helzie," she said when at first he didn't move, "I've had enough of your company for the night."

He blinked. "You'd set me out in the middle of nowhere, just for spite?"

"Two miles from the Freystane to your sister's pub," she clipped, glaring at the headlamp splash on the stone. "You're not too drunk nor too ill to walk that far."

"But..." he set his hand to the latch, but didn't pull it. "My boat. How—"

"That's never your boat, and we both know it," she rounded on him, crowding him into the door with a merciless pointing finger. "I saw Jane Embry's name engraved on the oarlocks. She'd no more give you leave to take it than I'd invite you to Sunday supper!" The wind gusted from the sea, clearing the dust from the air, and making the great stone keen softly above them. Helzie glanced up at it, swallowing hard. "Now get out," Mairead said again. "I'll take it back to her place, and if you take care not to vex me further, I might even not tell her, or Ben Skerrien, who it was that nicked it in the first place!"

Invoking the constabulary was, apparently, the key. Durn popped the door and slithered out onto the road quick as an eel, looking sour and spiteful between the headlamps and the setting moon. "This en't over," he said.

"Oh, it is," Mairead assured him. "Because you've gone and scared them off now. The seals'll not come back to the holm now they know the likes of you are lurking around to make off with one of their own. Not for a dozen years or more!"

"There's one that'll have to," he said, teeth flashing. "I got her skin—"

"And I threw it back into the sea, where it belongs," she lied, hoping he was too drunk or too angry to spot the flawed logic. The Freystane sang again in the shocked silence that followed.

Then, "You didn't! You bloody cow!" Face purpling with rage, Durn lurched forward, but Mairead leaned over and hooked the door out of his reach with a bang.

"So you go on and tell the old uncles down the tavern that you went hunting for an old wivey's tale down the Selkeness holm, and that I went and stole your luck," she cried, heart banging at her breast. "You just try it, and see if they believe it better than any other of your tales. All Ramphollow knows you for a liar, a lofter, and a sot who stays home while better men go off to war."

Then she keyed the engine to life with a roar, cranked the wheel, and drove the man from the road in a spray of gravel that was not half so spiteful as she really felt.

It was nearly four by the time Mairead made it back to the lighthouse. The sea wind was freshening up in anticipation of the coming dawn, but the night was still clear and fine when she pulled the old truck into the shed and turned its engine off.

She sat for a moment and faced the truth head-on, letting the smells of salted wood, diesel, and despair settle around her in the gloom. She'd never see the seals again. Her seals, for hadn't she gone to watch them dance in human skin every fine moon-graced night since she'd turned sixteen? Hadn't she guarded their secret, breathed no wondering word, and led no following eye to their private spot? Not even her brothers, who'd seen through her every ruse, had ever learned this one that she had loved all these furtive years. The seals gone now, and she'd told Helzie the truth of it; they wouldn't ever come back to the holm to dance again.

Damn the man for his greed!

She wrenched the door open, jammed the keys over the visor, and then kicked it closed with all the savagery she could muster. It wasn't as satisfying as she'd hoped—the anger was giving way now, realization setting in.

What need to comb the almanacs in search of clear weather now? Why bother to hold her breath when the moon swelled, to hope that the clouds might lift and call them in to shore just one more time before the winter? Why augur the storms and calms in the passage of sea-birds, fish, or beetles now that a clear night would bring her nothing more than stars? What would she look forward to now her one bit of magic in a gray-sky island life was at an end?

Or nearly at an end, anyhow.

A velvet tickle beneath her shirt reminded her as she turned up the path to the lighthouse proper. The lame girl's pelt, her private lie, and the secret she hardly dared consider. She would find a way to give it back somehow, as she'd promised herself out upon the holm. She'd realized then and there that she daren't just throw it into the sea. The tide would have swept the precious pelt inland up the river mouth, and into the hatchery nets. Or worse, all the way to the shipyard. The poor girl would never find it then.

Mairead shivered at the thought of that dark-eyed selkie girl shackled to some sooty dockside welder with knuckles like conkers and a temper to match. No. Never, if she could help it. Never.

She slipped two fingers beneath her coat, wormed them between buttons of her oversized shirt, and stroked the dense, silky pelt for a moment. "Come and find it," she said aloud to the wind scraping in from the sea. "Come find me. I'll keep it safe till you do." Then the light flashed round overhead, reminding her of her duties, and with a sigh Mairead squared her shoulders and headed for the lighthouse's kitchen door.

She was overdue for the fuel check by about two hours, but the reserve tank held enough to see the light through till dawn. She flipped the shunt and topped off the main tank all the same. She checked temperature gauges, then rested her head against the shaft housing to listen to the rumbling heartbeat of the engine that kept the light sweeping sunwise over the sea. It was steady, as measured as the soberest drummer; there was no grind of dust in the gears, no counterpoint tick of metal heating too fast, no squeal of dry shafts rubbing. The turning engine snored along peacefully, and after a moment or two longer than her reassurance strictly needed, Mairead pulled herself away from its lulling song and climbed the stairs into the house proper.

The bulkhead door shut out the engine's song, but the vibrations, as always, carried through the kitchen floor, chiming two glasses in the open cupboard until she nudged them apart on her way to the parlor stairs. At the landing, she paused by the window to watch until the light's sweeping beam caught the painted side of the *Ursilla Meur*, still moored off the jetty, her masts stepped, her sails neatly tied, and her rescue boats tenting the decks with strong-sloping keels to the sky. Just as Deen, Tam, and Jean had set her before they'd left the islands for war; waiting faithful as a dog for her man to come at need or whim and lead her from shore.

Mairead turned from the window and went to check the man hadn't died while she'd been out.

"Da?" she called as she opened the bedroom door, letting him hear her voice and go on sleeping, rather than wake in fear at her quiet steps beside the bed. She'd moved his service rifle from under his bed to the linen cupboard by the stairs so she wasn't in much danger, but still. There was no telling when her father would muster the strength to get up and about the place, or what his delirium would suggest he get into with nobody near to stop him. Just yesterday she'd returned from cleaning the lamp and mirrors in the tower to find the old man on hands and knees in the pantry cellar, digging up the dirt floor with his fingernails. Tonight, though, his thin, thready snore wove through the room unchecked, unobstructed, and she allowed herself a smile. Mansie Meur hadn't left the world just yet.

He grunted and tried to roll over in his sleep, fretting under the blankets until she caught his bird-thin shoulders and helped him along. "I'm here, Da," she told him, settling the bedding over him and pressing his pillow clear of his nose and mouth. "I'm home. It's all right."

The glass of water she'd left beside his bed was still full, but the whiskey he insisted upon by way of medicine was empty and dry. She kissed his temple and headed down the hall, thinking wistfully of just shucking her kit and falling straight into bed to sleep herself out.

Mairead knew better though. Tense, fractious, and smelling of sweat, rust, kelp, and blood, there was no way she could sleep. She didn't even want to imagine touching clean sheets without a good scrub first, so she passed her own door and went on instead to the bathroom at the far end of the hallway. There, she turned the taps and set about stripping down while the tub filled, tossing her damp socks and Jean's old flannel shirt into the hamper. She considered her dungarees for a long moment before consigning them there as well.

Unwrapping the sealskin, she set it carefully on the vanity as she stripped away the rest of her smalls and tried to ignore the sticky state of the underpants. She couldn't leave the pelt alone for long though. Its velvet gray folds shone in the light, luring her fingers in to stroke, then to pet, then to knead the dense fur.

How could it be so soft when it spent so long in the harsh brine? Bespelled, she lifted it to her face, shivering as the long, heavy folds draped along her breasts and belly. How could it smell so rich and warm, like smooth skin and clean sweat, and not at all like fish and piss and rotting weed? Her searching fingers found the facemask, long whiskers bristling against her thighs, nose a cool spot of pebbled leather in the hollow of her hip. Mairead took a shaking breath, closed her eyes, and smoothed the fur tight against her skin.

God, how she would miss it. The dancing, yes; the flash of limbs in the moonlight, lovely girls pale as foam and plump as plums, their dark hair glimmering as they danced under the moon, but later. Oh, later. When they danced in pairs and threes, tangled like driftwood in a restless tide. They kissed and stroked and sported themselves without a lick of shame, and dear God how she'd watched and yearned for their ease. For the way each chose whom they wanted, whether man or maid, and no bitter old priest appeared to shame them for the joy they took together.

Another shuddering breath—one that rubbed her breasts fiercely against the thick, furry nap, and drove her fingers down past the realm of pretense to stroke at her own sex even as her thumb rubbed circles around the sealskin's empty lips. It wasn't a sin for them. It wasn't a horrid obscenity, and proof of moral dissolution for them, as it was for the likes of her. They'd never face a village full of scorn and smirks for it. They'd never weather slights that struck like pitiless stones. They did not have to live on the island, with no escape from those smoke-dried, strangling moralities. Their secret was the where only, never the what.

Her lot was not theirs, and she knew it could not be, but... oh dear God, but draped in that lush, musky borrowed freedom, Mairead couldn't resist one last pretense. She settled to the toilet seat, one foot propped up high on the tub's rim to spread herself to the humid air. They'd done it thus: fingers teasing, slipping gentle and swift through skin as slick and wet as the sea, curling and tracing and diving deep. She bit her lip, turned a cry into a whimper, then added another finger and did it again. The pelt slid, whiskers scraping a delicious streak of pain across her exposed nub until she gasped and clutched it higher. One leathery flipper draped by chance across her gasping mouth, its scars rough and hushing against her lips. She could feel the nose just at her belly, whiskers pricked, as though her lovely girl were watching, rapt and hungry as Mairead delved and stroked and wrenched release from herself with her spindly human hands.

She bit the scarred flipper as she came, the taste of salt and dust filling her mouth even as sparks and tears filled her eyes. Her sex spasmed against her fingers like a wounded thing. A moment; two breaths scraped past the pain lodged in her throat, and then Mairead became aware of two things at once.

First, that the tub was brim-full and about to swamp the bathroom with tepid water. She lunged with a curse to twist the taps closed and yank the plug from the drain. Flood forestalled, Mairead allowed her thoughts to turn to the second thing.

Her memory would not serve; she had to see. Bundling herself into a towel, Mairead slipped back down to the window on the stairway landing, peering hard into the darkness until the great light swept it briefly away. But no, there was nobody out there, and nowhere for a selkie girl to hide in the lighthouse's wide and windswept garden. She'd imagined the voice, and the short, sharp cry matching hers as she'd spent under her own hands.

She'd wished it so, wished the selkie near to her passion; no less deluded herself than the old man asleep down the hall.

A sorry little madness, but honestly come-by, for what small comfort that could be.

When Ben Skerrien came round to the Selkeness light the next day, Mairead wasn't surprised. Annoyed, yes, but hardly surprised. The old Irishman had a sense of duty long as a trawler's lines, and it was doublesharp now the younger men of the island had lighted off and left the Law in his care alone.

He was a good man, and a fair one, if a little inflexible in his ideas of what was just and right, and honestly the village was lucky to have him willing to come out of retirement to do his bit. Still, watching the tall man come striding down the path to the shingle wall, Mairead found herself wishing with annoyance that the ferrylouper could remember that he was not actually one of them: that coming to the isles to fish and get fat in his twilight years didn't make Skerrien an Orkneyman any more than going to a St. Paddy's Day's piss up in Belfast made one of them Irish. That there were things the islands taught a body over a lifetime that couldn't be picked up in a few easy years of fishing off the harbor jetty, and the picking up of an empty uniform when the need arose.

Still, she rose to meet the man, brushing mortar off her fingers to shake his hand. "Ben."

"Miss Meur," he said, letting go quickly and brushing his own hand after. She hid a smile, and was glad of it when he gave a nod at the patch she was mending in the shingle wall. "That's tidy work there," he said. "Shall I wait inside while you finish it up?"

She shook her head, drew a lap of canvas over her mortar bucket and weighted it down with a large stone. "No need. This bit's got to dry the day before I can skim it with the final coat and paint it. Otherwise the first storm after a freeze'll have it out whole and bring the wall down besides."

"Oh," he said, and Mairead wondered if the startled look he swallowed was at the potential damage to the wall, or at her being competent to judge it and mend it right. After a moment though, he caught his wits and squared his jaw. "Well then, I suppose if you don't mind, we might talk a bit about what passed between you and Durn Helzie last night."

"Durn Helzie had no business coming round here," she said, gathering up her mortarboard and trowel to rinse them off at the tideline.

Ben followed, but stopped well back on the shingle. "So he was here then. And did you assault him with a stolen oar as well?"

She turned an outraged look on him as she slung brine and sand from the trowel's edge. "And is that what Helzie told you then? That it was me who stole that boat he turned up in last night? And I suppose he told you why he'd come creeping round while he knew my Da was too ill to run him properly off, did he?"

Ben shook his head, grave and stern. "No, Miss Meur, he didn't. When I spoke to young Mr. Helzie, he said he couldn't remember a thing about last night, and from the look of the bandages on him, it seemed he'd good reason to be forgetful."

"Aye, if you call not having to give an account of himself a good reason!" Mairead sneered. "There's nothing wrong with Helzie's memory, nor with his head unless he went and did something stupid after I ran him off here last night. You just ask for a look under those bandages and see if there's good cause for them at all!"

"Mrs. Embry reported that her son's boat was moved last night," Ben went on, following her up the shingle to the garage, "One of the oars did appear to be damaged a bit. So let's have it straight, Miss Meur. Did you steal the Embry's boat and wallop young Durn with the oar?"

"Is it straight you're wanting it, or just simple?" she challenged, putting the tools on their shelves with more force than was strictly necessary. "Because I can tell you that Durn stole that boat, which is straight and true, and I can tell you I took it back where it belonged last night, which is straight and true as well. So did I assault him with a stolen boat oar? Well I suppose I did at that, but you just ask yourself why before you point your glower at me, if you please."

"Suppose you just tell me why," he answered, stepping aside with a sweeping gesture toward the house.

"It's because he knows my Da's not well and my brothers are away, and he thinks he can come and make free with anything that's to his liking," she ground out, blinking fiercely to keep the angry tears back. "And when I instruct him otherwise—when I defend what's mine, he goes whimpering to you about it, and says he can't remember what happened, but surely I'm to blame?" Damn her eyes, why did she have to weep when she wanted to spit with rage? Why did tears always turn her anger soft and soppy and silly? Mairead dashed her cheeks dry, and stormed up the path to the house.

Ben followed, his measured strides sedate, and long enough to keep up with hers, though he didn't seem to hurry at all. That was warning enough for Mairead—she was as trimmed in by the truth of things as Durn. More so, truth be told, as she was a woman, unmarried and without prospects, and setting her word against that of a man who knew better than most how to play for sympathy. She took a deep breath as she fetched out her key at the kitchen door, and resolved to be merciless.

"You keep it locked even when you're about the place?" Ben asked as she slipped the key in and turned it. His face was amused, but not wholly inclined to laugh once he met her sober stare. "Most folk on these islands don't take the trouble."

"After last night, I hardly dare leave any door unlocked," she said, perversely grateful now for the wetness of her eyes, if a little shame-faced to see Ben's hardness soften as he noted it. "Come in and have a seat. I'll put the kettle on."

He did, and if his thoughtful silence followed her about the light-house kitchen, Mairead tried not to let it rattle her. She had the right of it, and if the truth whole wouldn't serve her, that didn't mean she had to lie. Let that be Helzie's trick—he'd more experience with it, after all. She held her own silence until the kettle sang, and kept it through the tidy, civilized dance of cups and saucers, milk and sugar, spoons and a few biscuits. When she finally sat down to pour the tea, it was Ben Skerrien who looked ruffled and unsure of himself.

"His sister's in a state, Miss Meur," he told her as he accepted the cup. "Mrs. Crimmon said he came home bloodied and half dead last night as she was closing the pub down. Says he'll have to be taken to the hospital down on Hoy, lest he die in his sleep, and won't hear a word Dr. Kerrow has to say about it. She's stirring up an awful fuss, and you must understand I do have to inquire."

"Yes, I do," she said, every word as calm as a cup of tea. "And as I've said, I did hit him with an oar last night."

His shaggy eyebrows went up, not in surprise, but perhaps in exasperation. "Good lord, girl, whatever for?"

"He got fresh with me, and I didn't like it," she replied, giving a shiver as she remembered the cunning glitter in his eyes just before he came at her.

That made the constable's eyebrows go slantwise. "Fresh? So you clipped him one with an oar?"

Mairead unbuttoned her cuff and slid back her flannel sleeve to show a nice line of bruises along her inner forearm. They could have been made by an angry grip, or perhaps the rail of an unbalanced dinghy being loaded into a truck without any help. She let Ben draw his own conclusions, saying only, "I very much did not like it."

Ben gently took hold of her wrist, urged it toward the watery sunlight coming through the window, and peered close. His hand was warmer than she'd expected, and while callused, surprisingly tender on her skin. "This is quite a bang," he said, looking up with concern. "Tell me, did he come down here without his boots on?"

She blinked, then thought for a moment. "Yes, now I think on it. His shoes were in the boat when I found it, but he had them when I drove him back to town and returned the boat. Why, has he lost them again?"

"Not that I know of," Ben answered, still holding her arm. "It's just I had a brief look 'round before I came to find you on the shingle, and there were footprints at the parlor windows. Footprints, not bootprints. Seemed odd that a man should come courting without his boots on," he mused, then flashed Mairead a startled glance when she yanked away.

"That was never any 'courting'," she said frostily, rolling down her sleeve. "That was a man who didn't want the creaking of his Wellies to give him away as he came where he wasn't welcome!"

"And why would he do such a thing? Has he taken a sudden fancy to you? He never seemed keen before."

"I'm sure I don't know," she replied with anger shaking her voice, and tearing up her eyes again, "but I suppose it wasn't much different to why any man does it; because he fancies he can, and no one will stop him." She reached for her teacup again, and let her hand tremble as she took a long drink. "Well, I stopped him properly, and I'll ask no man's pardon for it."

"Well then," Ben sighed after a long, considering moment, "well then. And I suppose you'll be wanting to file a complaint against him for it?"

Carefully, girl, she warned herself when she glanced up to find the constable's eyes shuttered and blank as an empty sky. "I see no point to it, so long as he'll keep himself away from here, and from me," she answered. "There's no witnesses to what happened, nobody to testify for either of us, and so why waste a judge's time with it when nothing will be done anyhow? Just warn him off our lands, and let that be enough. The war won't go on forever, and once my brothers are home, he'll be much better behaved, I'm sure."

He cut a glance at her again, clearly dubious, but Mairead merely drained her cup and reached for the pot again. "Can I top you up before you go?"

"No, thank you," he said with a smile so sudden he might have conjured it. "It's a long and bumpy drive back up to the village though, so if you don't mind...?"

Mairead let herself chuckle, and rose to wave him toward the bathroom up the stairs. "By all means. And Da might be awake by now as well, if you'd like to pop in and say hello."

"And is he better then?" There, at last, was concern she did not doubt. Mansie Meur was a friend to every man in Ramphollow, and his sudden decline after his three treasured sons went off to the war was a point of pain, regret, and gossip to many.

She shook her head. "The same. Dr. Kerrow says there's nothing to be done now, but to wait and see what it is he decides he'll do."

Ben shook his head, and tucked his cap under his elbow as he mounted the stairs. "The papers tell of new miracles of medicine and science every day, and still a strong man can die of a broken heart with no cure to be had," he tsked. "Well, there are more things in Heaven and Earth, Horatio, and all that, I suppose."

"Aye," she answered as he went up, but she was thinking of thick, short fur against her skin, bare feet in the garden bed beneath the window, and a short, sharp cry in the moonless dark. She cast a glance at the pantry, and the great enameled pot she only pulled out for soups in the winter. Its lid didn't quite lay flush, and could she see the fine sheen of fur through that crack? Not safe, not secret. Not even with the doors locked, and Da dozy with the whiskey in his bedroom.

She had to think of something better.

Mairead moved the skin to six different hiding places over the course of that long morning. Behind the kerosene tanks in the cellar; at the bottom of her laundry hamper; inside one of her mother's embroidered pillowcases at the top of the linens closet; beneath the truck's splitting seat; behind Deen's collection of repair manuals and Jean's adventure stories in their dusty, desolate room.

But every time she tried to get about her chores, the worry for it haunted her, nibbled and nagged at her, until she had to go back to wherever she'd left the thing, just to be sure of it. At last, disgusted at how like a broody hen she was being, Mairead gave up and wrapped the seal pelt tightly to her skin, bulking out her ribs beneath the swell of her breasts.

If she'd been doing anything more girlish than tending lines, mending her traps, and hoeing up weeds from the garden, she might have thought twice about the bulk it added to her normally skinny frame. But she'd taken to wearing her brothers' castoffs for her chores years ago, and since they'd gone away the chores were so frequent it hardly seemed worth the time to put on skirts or dresses. If anything, the sealskin made her work clothes fit a bit better. And having it against her skin meant Mairead wasn't forever clucking and hovering over the silly thing in search of a better place to hide it.

It also meant she spent the day flustered and pink, taut with arousal, guiltily enjoying the soft pelt's caress against her breasts, and looking over her shoulder to be sure no townies had come round who might wonder at the state of her. Her luck held though, and she spent the day alone with her bait, her pliers and wire, her hoe, and her decidedly improper urges.

It was her stomach, finally, that informed her of the lateness of the hour, for the pale summer sky held no inkling of twilight, even though her watch claimed that eight o' clock had come and gone.

With a grimace, she set the rake over her shoulder and turned to take it back to the shed, but a flicker of white at the corner of her eye brought her lurching about to stare up the hill to the house instead.

Mairead traced the familiar lines of her only home with a suddenly wary eye; the long box of the house, its white walls going pink in the lowering sunlight, its tin roof straight and square, its double row of windows tall, narrow, and closed every one. Its door still closed tight. At the seaward side of the house, the lighthouse tower loomed, twice again the height. Not so much as a sea bird moved on the tower's walkway, nor did anything but the wind move in the gardens around her. There was nothing to see. Even the steep path threading up the ridge to the headland, and the only road into Ramphollow, was empty. Nothing was there.

Except that something was there.

A flicker of white, twenty feet up the tower wall, so quick and fluid she'd have missed it blinking. Clutching the rake, Mairead circled the house as silently as booted feet could go, hardly breathing, eyes held wide lest she miss the movement again.

She did not miss it. The lazy evening wind lifted the curtains out of the open casement of the window at the stairway landing, fanning them out over the wall like a child's MayDay ribbons. Mairead felt her heart seize up tight at the sight of it, and of the trellis below, pulled loose of its tethers and hanging askew, dripping scarlet rose petals like blood on the grass below. Then she dropped the rake in the drive and ran for the house with all her speed.

She hit the front door at a run, fumbling furiously with the screen, her keys, and even the damned latch until she could fling it wide at last; but the sight inside stopped her cold. The parlor was a mess of upturned cushions, tipped baskets, and emptied drawers. Every piece of furniture in the place had been tipped or rifled, and the old braided rug bunched up to show the plank floor beneath. Even the firebox had been searched, kindling and coals strewn across the hearthstone like a witch's knucklebones.

Through the kitchen doorway, Mairead could see the cupboards and drawers askew, pots and utensils in disarray. The great stockpot lay on its side on the floor against the opened door to the cellar. She could hear the grind of the engines over her thundering heart, could smell the kerosene, diesel, and grease overlooming the common kitchen scents of shellfish, onions, and bread—all, familiar, but none at all comforting in the long evening light.

"Helzie," Mairead growled, catching up the iron hook from the fire set and heading for the cellar. "If you've touched the engines, I swear..." But even as she kicked the sofa cushions out of her path, Mairead heard a murmur from above her head—a creak of the old floorboards, a rustle of bedsprings, one voice questioning and low, answered with her father's thin, fretful tenor.

He's got at Da! She bolted for the stairs at once, heart thudding at her ribs as though it wanted out, rage locked tight with fear in the thick of her throat.

Her bedroom, the bath and linen cupboards, the boys' rooms; she took in their pillaged state in at a glance as she passed. Her own, she barely noted, had been ransacked with particular enthusiasm, rendering the once-familiar landscape bizarrely alien against the twilight shadows.

"You leave him be!" she cried, skidding into her father's bedroom on the hallway rug, and gouging the door as she brandished the firehook, "He's done nought to..." But then the words died in her throat, the rage and fear suddenly whelmed in a wash of an intense, awkward emotion she could hardly fathom. For there at her father's side, red eyed, rumpled, and entirely beautiful in Tam's old grotty toweling robe, sat the seal girl.

Her seal girl. Sitting there on Da's mattress with a bowl on her knees, and a spoon halfway to the old man's open lips, just as though she fed him to his health every day. She half turned as Mairead came in, cast her a single anguished glance, and then turned back to her task with a tiny sigh.

Mairead stared, throat wound so tight around her confusion that she couldn't even begin to speak. The seal girl's feet were bare and grimy, the left's scars gleaming through rose briar scrapes and beach pebble bruises. Her hair was dry now, treacle-colored in the lamplight where the moon and the sea had always before made it seem black. It tumbled thick and long and threaded with gold against the borrowed blue stripes. "Nearly done," the girl said, catching up a drop of soup from Da's lip, so Mairead couldn't guess to which of them she spoke.

"You came." The words were out of her mouth before she could consider them.

"I had to," the selkie replied, setting spoon to bowl with a neat click, and laying the both on the night table beside the empty whiskey glass. Her gaze lingered on the lamp, as though the shine could hide the sorrow looming in her eyes. "Are you hungry?" she said after a moment, gathering herself to rise. "There is more soup in the kitchen."

Mairead glanced back at the stairs, confused. "The... but you've wrecked the—"

"Mairey?" Da asked from the bed, his brows lowering to peer at her, "Is that you?"

"I had to search," the girl said without a glance at her erstwhile patient. "Don't worry, I'll set it all straight again. You should eat something."

Mairead shook her head. "You don't... it's all—"

"Who are you?" Da bit out, his eyes suddenly clear and fierce as he wrestled with the bedding to try and shove himself upright. "You're never my Scilla! What do you mean, coming in here and—"

"It's all right, Da," Mairead rushed to calm him, trying not to notice how the seal girl flinched out of her way as she went to her father's side. "She isn't Mum, but she's all right. She won't hurt you."

"She don't belong here!" he fretted, catching at Mairead's hands. "You tell her!"

"I know," she soothed, leaning the firehook against the night table to try and settle him. "And she won't be staying, I promise."

"You know I can't leave," the girl replied, her smooth voice knotting just a little, as though she'd practiced saying it until the words didn't choke her. "Not without my skin."

The skin. No sooner was it named, then Mairead became exquisitely aware of its bulk against her ribs, of the prickle where hairs pressed cross-grain to her skin, a sweaty snug of leather where one flipper stuck to her back. She took a deep breath, and shivered as the skin seemed to twitch around her. "I... I know." Another breath, a moment's pause while she smoothed her father's downy hair away from his face, a handful of heartbeats while she wondered what the devil she was waiting for. And then she stood up straight, squared her shoulders, and turned around.

"I know," she said, and began to unbutton her shirt. The girl gave a yelp, ragged and rough when the flannel fell away, revealing silver fur. She lurched a half step before stopping herself with a shiver, eyes welling, fist pressed against her lips as she watched Mairead unwind the pelt from around herself. She looked terrified, furious, and it was only as the pelt came away, and let her sweaty skin prickle in the cold that Mairead realized how things must seem. "No," she said, "It's not— I mean I'm not going to—"

"That's not yours!" Da's voice shocked Mairead around, the skin clutched reflexively before her naked breasts. Somehow he'd slipped free of the bedclothes and caught up the firehook, though he could barely brandish it as he tottered toward her. "You haven't any right! You give it back at once!"

"I'm giving it back, Da," she said, hastily thrusting the skin in the girl's direction with one hand as she snatched the firehook from her father with the other. "It's all right, I'm just—"

The girl jerked her pelt free of Mairead's grip, one of its claws scoring along her arm as it went. The firehook dropped to the floor between Mairead's feet, bouncing painfully off her shin. Her father lunged at her with a scream.

"You give it back to me!"

"Go!" She shouted to the seal girl, as over they went in a tangle of nightshirt, knees, and elbows, Mansie Meur battling with all his waning frenzy while Mairead struggled to contain his thrashing without doing any real harm.

It took only minutes for the fight to wane, and for Mansie's rage to witter away into panting, weeping confusion once more. But that was long enough for the seal girl to escape with what was hers. Mairead tried not to wonder, as she wearily put her father back to bed, if the beautiful girl with the sad dark eyes had paused on the shingle for even one backward glance. Or had she taken her freedom with both hands instead and run with all her might?

In her place, Mairead thought she knew which she herself would have done.

For that night, and much of the following day, Mairead slept. She stirred up only to see to the light's maintenance, and once to her father, who had used her quiet distraction as an opportunity for mischief, and taken a notion to fetch down something from the top of the old armoire. He pulled the thing over on himself with a mighty crash, and when Mairead came running to his cries, he called her by her mother's name.

Of course, then he shouted at her for snooping and insisted he'd been robbed, though he couldn't say of what. He bawled that she was breaking his arm when she tipped the cabinet up off him, and then tried to wallop her with an old slipper when she helped him out of the tumble of clothes and loose drawers afterward. She almost wished she could just leave him lying there in the mess he'd made, but spite just took too much energy, so she took his slipper away instead.

She was nearly two hours getting him calmed, cleaned, and settled back to bed, where he watched her tidy away his mess with eerily sharp eyes. He didn't make a peep while she sorted his clothes back to their drawers, hung the musty shirts and trousers he'd not worn in months, and tucked his shoes two by two along the bottom. She was just hunting down the mate to an old Wellington boot she'd found half under the bed when Mansie Meur broke his silence at last.

"Mairey," he said, the firm-voiced ghost of his younger self startling her around with a gasp. "Mairey, you should sell the boat."

"I should..." She took a breath, and tossed the lonely boot into the armoire before shutting it. "But Da, why would you sell the *Ursilla*? She's safe at her mooring, and the boys'll surely want her for the cod run when they're back from the—"

"It's dangerous," he cut her off. "Who knows what could happen if you tried to take her out."

"And why would I do that? I've never even gone out on her but that Tam or the twins took me," she answered, still baffled, and no little alarmed at his sudden lucidity. "I'd hardly know how to turn her nose and slip the lines—"

"I won't have it! The boat's to go, I tell you! You find a buyer and get a decent price for her, or I'll scuttle her in the Scapa Flow, and let her keep company with the German fleet!"

"Da, there's a war on!" The calm tone failed her at last. "There'll be no buyer for a boat like her. Nobody's buying so much as a pot if they can patch what they already have!"

"I'll do it!" He rose to meet the challenge in her voice, struggling up out of the bedclothes again, eyes bulging and fists knuckled white. "I'll sink her, I swear it, I will!" And then it was the old, familiar struggle of Mansie against his own weak wits, weaker body, the bedclothes, gravity, and his well-meaning daughter.

The pitched battle lasted until a flying elbow sent the whiskey decanter toppling across the bed. By the time Mairead had mopped up the spill, changed the sheets, and set the room right again, her father had forgot the whole thing, and merely wanted to know about having cod and chips for his tea.

There wasn't any, nor did she feel up to making the meal, but he was happy enough with the bowl of soup Mairead brought him. And when he nodded off over his empty bowl, she took it for the blessing intended, and slipped off for another nap herself.

And thus went the pattern of her days, measured against the

consistent, predictable needs of the tower, engine, and lantern, and the inconsistent whims of the old man down the hall. She kindled the lamp at twilight without fail, filled the engine's reservoirs, cleaned filters, scanned the radio for reports from the royal weather stations, and sounded the mournful horn when the cold sea mists rolled in to blanket the headland in sodden gray.

But aside from those tasks, she found she could make herself do very little. Her lobster pots went un-baited, weeds put up stealthy heads in her garden rows, and the final coat of mortar waited in its bucket beside the shingle wall. And Mairead slept on the bare mattress in her brothers' room, clearing paths through the wreckage in order to reach the necessities of toilet, kitchen, and stairway.

She did think, one or two times, that she had better get herself in hand and do something about the state of the place, but the notion never managed to take hold through the pall of weariness that had settled about her. She managed a bit of washing up, laundered some linens and got them hung, but never gathered them in from the lines.

Twice she dozed off at the radio, and woke herself with a start, thinking she'd heard her brother's voice behind her, a laughing goad to wake up and shift her silly arse... Channel chatter both times, but still her silly heart took ages to calm afterward. She told herself, glowering as sternly at the mirror as she could, that it wouldn't be any better if the boys were home. They'd always been more than half gone anyway, ranging far and wide as tomcats while she lurked shy and awkward at home, and ventured out only in their shadow.

They wouldn't help, were they on the island instead of out upon the seas, not really. They'd tease and heckle her into making a brave face, and they'd not suffer any of Helzie's disrespect, but there would have been no sympathy out of them—they weren't the type. But still she did not remove the photo from her nest, where she'd placed it to keep watch over her exhaustion, like mischievous guardian angels with better things to do.

Her father's ravings had gone sharp-eyed and frantic in the wake of the seal-girl's visit, and Mairead contained them as best she could. She promised to attend to whatever petty thing he set his attention upon, only to ignore it with relief as soon as his whiskey calmed the notion out of him again. She knew he needed better care, and promised herself that she would manage it soon. Soon, when she was better herself.

For she was ill—that was the only explanation for it. Seeing as how she'd no dutiful child of her own to wait hand and foot upon her comfort, Mairead found herself deciding again and again that the state of the house, and the niceties of nursing a mad and troublesome old man, could officially go hang. So long as the light came on, the horn sounded when needed, and her father was kept from hurting himself in his ravings, who but herself would even know if she were to roll the great, tumbled mess out the door and down to the sea, and leave the house empty and echoing?

The photo on her mattress kept her decent company, at least; Jean, Deen, and Tam, all trim, fine, and smart, grinning at their silly little Mairey and her dreams of fur and skin and deep, cold water. They'd never got sick in their lives, those three; never fell behind in any race; never, that she could tell, felt wee and weak, stupid, awkward and shy. They had roared through island life like princes, knowing all fine things as their due, and carrying Mairead along, blinking and stunned in their local celebrity. She'd never much wanted it, but had known better than to spoil the show for its stars, and so she had always put on a good try. And even now, those three expectant, cheery smiles prompted Mairead to summon up the will to rise from the bed, find some clothes, and at least make a show of things when morning kept on coming.

The fugue couldn't last, of course. She was an island girl, not some spoilt city flower come up for the summer nights and Beltane fires. Mairead had been raised on hard work and horse sense, not self indulgence and moping about while the days went begging. The Orkney men were gone defending the Crown, after all, and those left behind owed it to them to take up the slack until they could come home. So, come the week's end, Mairead found herself binding up her hair, rolling up her sleeves, and setting her brothers' rooms to rights again.

She turned the beds out to air on the landing, pounded the pillows, and shook the sheets and blankets as though they held the last slivers of her smashed fancies. The piles of trophies, plaques, and prizes took a dusting, as did their shelves. Even the cache of her brothers' pin-up magazines, so very influential and instructive in Mairead's own childhood, went back into the bedframes in stacks of three or fewer, lest they skew the sheets once the beds were made up.

The other photos, the ones Mairead privately thought of as the "hopefuls," she swiped into the bin without a second glance. None of those Ramphollow girls had held her brothers' attention for long, and the fact that none of them bothered to keep touch now the Mansie boys were away stood for proof that they all of them knew it. Let the simpering, flirting creatures maintain their own fictions—Mairead had enough to concern her already. Anyway, she didn't care for all those flat, hollow smiles watching her work.

She cleaned the kitchen that night, finishing off the last of the soup, and scrubbing the room from tin to tiles, and every dish between them. The light's engine pulsed and ground beneath her feet while she worked, reminding her with its ceaseless hum that the important things did not change; night came, storms rose, and ships needed warning away from the rocks that would break their unwary hearts. The light had been enough to keep her father going once her mum had died, that much she knew from Ramphollow's gossips—and who was she to demand a greater share?

Tomorrow, she told herself, standing outside the front door, and watching the lingering glow of the sky as the sun tiptoed just beneath the horizon. Tomorrow, she would use the kitchen to cook. She would tackle the parlor, dining room, bath, and her own bedroom, get all the laundry out and hanging, and finally see to the patch down on the shingle wall. It would be a relief to get about things, surely—to shake the droop from her spine, and let honest work in the damp sea air pry loose the knot of loss around which her heart had been struggling to beat for days.

"Tomorrow," she said aloud: to herself, to the shrouded sun, to all the days that stretched out before her. "I'll do it tomorrow. First thing, for sure." Then she went upstairs, to the radio room near the top of the tower, where the light's heat baked down through the stone ceiling and banished all trace of chill, even in the dampest of days. There she settled into the chair with the headphones pillowing her head, and let the ghosts of the empty airwaves sing her to sleep.

Mairead woke to the sound of a horn. Not the deep-throated, bone-shaking roar the tower sang out when fogs lifted in from the sea, nor yet the tinny honk of an auto; this was the steamy, ringing note that could only be a boat underway. And very close by. That realization drove the cobwebs from her thoughts, and brought Mairead's feet smartly to the floor.

Dashing to the tiny window, she pressed close to stare, and then to curse as she spotted the craft, a well-loved and cheerily blue fisher, puffing away as her captain turned her in toward a mooring just alongside the shrouded Ursilla Meur. The stack let off another white-breathed puff of song, loud enough to make the glass buzz under Mairead's fingers, and she turned to run for the stairs.

"Mairey?" Mansie called, timorous and confused as she thundered down past his room. "Mairey, what's wrong? What's happened?"

"It's only Aunt Jenn, Da," Mairead shouted back without stopping. "I'm going out to help her with the lines, so don't make a fuss." If he made any reply, Mairead couldn't hear it through the rattle of her feet on the stairs. Skidding into the parlor, she spared a moment's horrified despair for the state of things, but the horn sounded again, three short bursts like raps on a door that didn't stand a chance of staying closed. Mairead invoked Tam with a curse that had got him a thrashing when she was eleven. Then she dashed out the front door, down the shingle, and out the lighthouse's narrow jetty to meet the trim blue boat as she settled into place against the bumpers.

"You weren't still abed now, were you Mairey!" Jennie Towrie called, blowsy and stout, and still half swallowed in an oversized mac as she slung the heavy hawsers out over the forecastle. "I thought you might be taking sick yourself when you didn't come down the shop for supplies on Wednesday, and to look at you, I was right. You're beat, girl!"

Mairead shook her head, and wound the rope over the cleat to pull the *Fisher King* in close by the bumpers. "Late night with the generator," she lied, tying the bowline off then heading for the mid and aft lines to do the same. When she straightened from the task she found the old woman peering narrowly at her over the top of a crate of groceries, and regretted her fiction at once.

"Well then we'll just have a look at it once we get this lot stowed—"

"I got it sorted out though," Mairead protested, but took the crate all the same. "It was just a little fuel line problem. Fiddly, but not too hard. It's all set, and fine to carry on."

"All the same," Jenn said, and dropped two large duffels over the rail before hopping to the jetty herself, "Four eyes are sharper than two, and we can't have it going on the blink while we're all down the church, can we?"

"The church?" The words were out of her mouth even as she remembered. Emily Braeson. Her Gloucestershire airman about to ship out from the Scapa Flow base. The wedding Ramphollow had been in spasms over all spring. The wedding she'd forgot near as soon as she'd heard of it. Jenn's duffel bags suddenly took on a more sinister mien as Mairead backed a step. "I. That is, I don't—"

Jenn barked a laugh, and shouldered up both. "Have aught to wear. I know. You've been nicking your brother's trews since before they left home, and don't think I haven't noticed. And you've grown a pinch taller since spring as well. I doubt your old dancing clothes are like to do you any good, assuming the mice haven't got to them. Now trust your Aunt Jenn, dear. I'll have us both passing for ladies well before it's time to go." She chuckled, and hoisted one of the bags higher. "I daresay I'll even get Mansie turned out proper, if he's not drunk already."

"Da can't go," Mairead said, groceries rattling as she hurried to catch up. "He's worse than ever. And I don't think I should go either. The engine, you know. And I... I might be getting sick after all." She could hear the desperation in her voice, could hear how thin the lies lay, one over the other, could see them sliding off Jenn's shrewd gray gaze, but somehow she couldn't make herself stop talking. "You ought to go on without us tonight."

Jenn stood for a moment where the shingle curved up toward the house in a narrowing path. She rested her hip and one bag against the half-mended wall, and looked at Mairead as though she were hollow. "Bollocks," she declared after a moment, and turned briskly away up the path.

Mairead lurched after her, but the host of excuses crowding into her throat made it no farther than a yelp and a curse as she tripped over the mortar bucket, abandoned lo these many days, and had to scramble to keep from measuring her length in gravel, and strewing groceries all along the shingle. By the time she'd got her feet straight under her and squared the crate with gravity again, Jennie Towrie was already at the lighthouse door.

"Oh, Mairey," she said without turning as Mairead came up behind her on the doorstep at last. "What's happened, love?"

Looking in over Jenn's shoulder, seeing with fresh eyes the wreckage she'd nearly got used to in a week of ignoring it, Mairead couldn't blame the woman for her horror. "I... It's..." She swallowed, then set the crate down and tried again, barely managing a whisper. "I was looking for something, that's all. Couldn't find it. Got a bit carried away, and just—"

She stopped with a huff as Jenn turned about, dumped both bags off her shoulder, and caught Mairead into a hug. "Oh, my peedie girl," she crooned, petting at Mairead's hair with one hand while patting her like a colicky infant with the other. "Oh, poor lamb, you needn't tell your old Auntie Jenn stories, I promise."

It was on the tip of Mairead's tongue to protest when Jenn put her suddenly back at arm's length, and patted her cheek with a wiry hand. "I can't count the number of times I came out here and found your poor mam in just the same state, back before you was born. She'd get into such a lather when your da would be out on the lines, and she'd turn the house upside down and back to front looking for the silliest things. An old mac, or a kettle, or candlestick." She turned them both back to the house, her arm still looped behind Mairead's shoulders, too kind to call a prison as she drew the both of them in. "And not a friend did poor Ursilla have here on the island but me to help her set it right again before your da came home for his supper."

"But how," Mairead protested weakly as Jenn finally let go and set two of the dining room chairs upright, "how did you know when—"

"Oh, I came by all hours back then," she replied, pushing Mairead down to sit, then bustling back to the doorway to bring the baggage in. "Your da asked me to, at first. She was from Australia, of course, and hadn't the first notion of how to live, or keep a house here on the islands, so I said I'd look after her. And then of course, her being such a sweet creature, and so shy, why I came along just to have her company." She paused on her way to the kitchen with the groceries, to give Mairead a pat on the shoulder and a doting smile. "And when she left us, how could I love her wee little girl any less than my own dear friend? So don't you have a care for it, my girl. I've set this house aright before, and with less time than we've got today. I know the way of it."

From there onward, there was no argument to be had. Mairead protested her health, Jenn said they'd leave early enough to stop by Dr. Kerrow's on the way. Mairead protested Mansie's health, Jenn pointed out that Emily was counting on him to walk her down the aisle, since her own da was away with the army, and he as close as kin. It was when Mairead stooped to protesting the state of the lighthouse generator that Jenn put a stop to it.

"Mairead Amity Meur, you are going to this wedding. No, don't you talk back to me, girl, you just fold up those tablecloths and heed me well. I know you don't care much about Emily or her young man; I know you didn't get on with her at school, or her friends neither; and I know you don't like crowds or parties any more than your poor mother did, but we have a war on, girl!" Jenn punctuated her opinion with savage plumpings of the sofa pillows, not seeming to notice the billowing dust. "Our island boys are going away to die every day, and the Crown brings strangers in to live at the base for a month, or six, and they give a dance every once in awhile, then they're gone again too. And there's precious little left, with all of that, to bring us all together as we ought to be. But a wedding, Mairey. A ceremony of love, and of hope. What's that but a gift, even to us who only go to watch the vows said?"

A trial, Mairead thought, staring hard at the linen in her hands. *An ordeal with drinks and scones over thumbscrews afterward. And dancing.*

But aloud, she said only, "I don't want to go."

At which Jenn gave a smile that was all sympathy and warmth as she tossed the pillows into place. "No more do I, darling, but if we don't, Emily and her ma and aunties will all say we've kept off because we're jealous. And I don't know about you, but I'll be birched before I'll give those gossiping old cows the satisfaction!"

The key to getting through the evening, Mairead told herself, was to keep a drink in her hand whenever she could, keep moving, and to pretend she couldn't hear the whispers.

The first two tricks served to keep her well shy of the massive wedding cogs that were making the sunwise rounds of the guests—that is to say, the entire population of Ramphollow, along with every officer from the Scapa Flow base who could get leave to attend. So long as Mairead wasn't ever to the right of anyone who took possession of the cog, she wouldn't have to partake of the steaming, peppery brew of ale, gin, brandy, and whiskey. And so long as her full hand stopped her looking thirsty, she'd safely beg off any of the sailors pushing other drinks her way as well.

She'd drifted for most of the afternoon already, letting the townies shunt her to the rear of the procession as the Wedding March headed off from the church to the Braeson family's croftholding. She'd kept silent pace with the Tail Sweepers, smart and uncomfortable in the new dress and heels Aunt Jenn had brought for her. The crisply painful shoe prints she left were the last the Sweepers' big heather brooms brushed out of the road. Upon arriving at the croft, Mairead had taken the stew and scones they'd brought as gifts to Emily's mum, and then just let herself be swept up in the kitchen's business, picking her supper piecemeal from the platters rather than taking a seat at the gossiping tables outside.

The kitchen gossip wasn't much better, but handling the food meant she didn't have to stand very still in either company. Over the pots and plates, the talk was all of the bridegroom and his chosen mates, ferryloupers all, who hadn't the first notion of the Island's ways when it came to wedding, and who had shown a criminal disinclination to roll the poor man in treacle and trash on his Blackening Night, or to parade him drunk through a town full of laughing Orkneymen. Likewise, there had been a certain air of amusement upon the all-important foot washing night, which surely bode ill things for the match. Mairead kept to herself the suspicion that any man who married the likes of Emily Braeson was most likely quite fond of suffering, and wouldn't much mind the portended ill luck.

Instead, she loaded her hands with a platter of cakes and cream, and shouldered her way out into the main room's din. She found room for her burden on the sideboard, but no sooner had she set it down, than she turned to find Aunt Jenn behind her, looking tipsy, flushed, and irritated at once. "Well my girl, you were right about your da," she said, tipping a nod toward the fire nook across the room, where Mansie Meur seemed intent upon getting at something up the flue, despite the tidy summertime fire going there. Two of his friends were fending him off it, but only just, and it was clear the old man's temper was spinning up to a dither. "I'll have to take him home before he makes a scene, or takes his trousers off again."

"I'll just get the plates from the kitchen," Mairead said, relieved beyond the telling of it to have an excuse to go. Jenn's hand on her arm stopped her though.

"Oh no, dear. Pearl's made it a point to let me know how handy you're being in the kitchen," Jenn said, with a particularly cruel wink and smile. "And what with all of Emily's silly sisters already skived off to the barn, they can't possibly do without you now." She chucked a finger under Mairead's chin to nudge her mouth closed. "Price of competency, my dear. Let that be a lesson to you about volunteering. Now then, I've asked young Corporal Bonham there to bring you back out to the lighthouse later, once the dancing's wound down." She tipped a nod to a handsome fellow in the corner, all chin and ginger hair. He nodded back when he saw them looking, and Mairead whirled on her aunt before he did something horrid like smile and wave into the bargain.

"Aunt Jenn!"

"Oh, nonsense. I remember how you loved to dance, and it's high time you took a turn with a man who wasn't your brother. Now you needn't just go with him, you know. Lots of these navy boys who'll remember when you all used to go out to the monthlies at the Officer's club down the base, and they'll be keen for a girl who can dance the way you can."

She felt her face go cold just thinking of it. "I... I can't. With strangers? What if... what if they—"

"It's just a few dances, Mairey," Jenn said, just a little sad beneath the teasing, "not an engagement." Then Mansie's reedy voice rose briefly over the din, and she turned with a sigh. "I'd better go get him now. Don't you worry, I'll see that he's dosed down safe and proper. You just have a good time, love."

Though she might have pushed on, and stubbornly followed along with what little family she had on the island, Mairead found she just hadn't the energy for it. So instead, she took up a glass of whiskey as Jenn hustled her father out, slipped into a shadowed

corner behind the loaded trestles, and leaned up against the wall
to take a rest. The drink coated her tongue with fire, and the roar
of the merrymaking rolled around her, losing the distinction of
words after a time. If she closed her eyes, she could almost imagine
it was a flock of gigantic terns, clamoring over drying nets and
middens.

Almost.

"Salvage now, is it?" A laughing voice intruded on her musing,
"What bunk. And you say this poor Putnam bastard's keen to take
the bag?"

Mairead opened her eyes. Dr. Kerrow and Talin Embry drew up
to the sideboard, but neither spotted her as they refilled their plates
and cups. "Aye, so it seems," Talin replied, "and he won't hear ill
of his newfound friend, neither, so it's no good warning him and
his money clear of Helzie."

The doctor shook his head, not so amused as his friend. "You'd
think, him a navy man, he'd know better than to swallow the like.
If those old German fleet boats could be got, they'd have been got
already. No reedy Orkneyman with a half a notion and a glib tongue
can talk the wrecks out of the waves."

"Aye, well. Our Durn swears he's got a sure way to get at them
now, and if only he'd a good mate with deep pockets to go in with
him, why he'd make them both a bloody mint." Talin snorted, the
bitter experience of having been taken for a fool weighing heavily
in his tones. "There's none of us here in Ramphollow will give him
a hearing anymore, of course, so it's down at the base he's spending
his time and spinning his tales."

Dr. Kerrow sighed and took a scone as Talin knocked back his
drink. "Well, we can only hope poor Mr. Putnam can be shipped
off before he beggars his fortune on fool's gold."

"Aye. Or we'll all be lucky, and Our Helzie will get himself
pressed into service for his cheek. Then we'd be shut of his trouble
at last." Talin said, refilling his glass. "Why old Ben Skerrien's just
told me he's had to warn the man off from Mansie's old lighthouse.
Warrant he claimed it was 'salvage' he was about out there, as well.

And old Mansie not yet in his grave, let alone that girl of his married off or moved out of the place. It's a shame, it is."

"Talin," the doctor murmured, with a glance at Mairead's shadowy corner. Mairead sighed to herself and weighed her chances of getting away unseen. Many of her age mates had slipped out of the feasting room to join the dance in the barn, but between the gossiping pair, and the cluster of old menye singers taking up along the other end of the wall, she didn't like her odds much. Perhaps if she pretended she hadn't heard?

"You recall that business with our rowboat going missing last week?" Talin went on, oblivious as she fixed her eyes on the far wall. "Well it turns out Durn had taken it into his head to row out to the lighthouse with an eye toward—Oi! Oh..."

Well that would be it then. Mairead glanced over to find Talin Embry's face gone over all pink and mortified, and worse, the doctor looking solemn and sympathetic beside him. She set her drink aside as the fisherman recovered himself with a broad grin. "Why Miss Mairey, I was just telling Dr. Kerrow here how you went and brought our boat back after himself 'borrowed' it, unasked. Only it's you who'd make the better tale of it, couldn't you, seeing as how it was you who—"

"Seeing as how it was her who nearly killed him!" Cait Crimmon appeared at Embry's side, all towering dudgeon and calico as she slammed two tavern casks down onto the table. "And not satisfied with attempted murder, she goes on to slander Durn's good name as well!" She made a spitting noise. "Poacher? Thief? And more, I'll not say, as I'm a decent Christian with the sense to know a shameful lie when I hear it!"

Mairead stared at the wall behind the publican's shoulder, unable to stop her hand curling over her bruised arm. *I'll not answer* she told herself, aware that she was shaking, furious, and half wishing she had one of Talin Embry's oars to hand just now. *I'll not give her any words to twist...*

"How dare you show your face in this town after what you've done, Mairead Meur?" Crimmon pressed, as though scenting blood. "My brother's struggled all his life just to get along, and everyone knows he couldn't harm a fly—"

"Pfft. Pull t'other one," Embry put in, just enough whiskey in him to chin up when she rounded on him rather than giving way. "Anyone who's seen Helzie play on the school rugger team knows the boy's no frail, asthma or no. And he's well known for a lackworth around here, missus, so don't you go on saying he's not capable! Miss Meur's a fine looking girl, after all, and her lot's a good one, her bein' the only girl old Mansie ever had, so—"

"You hold your lying tongue, Talin Embry," she cried, the rage in her one finger shoving the man so hard against the trestle that the glasses rattled. "My Durn wouldn't look twice at a cheap little thing like that—"

"Now, Mrs. Crimmon," the doctor soothed.

"Like what?" It wasn't until all three had turned to stare that Mairead was aware she'd spoken aloud. But in the thick, shocked silence, she couldn't take the words back, so she repeated them. "Tell us all, Cait, just what kind of a thing you suppose I am, that your peedie wee brother couldn't possibly come sneaking around my home in a stolen boat? What sort of a thing do you mean to say? Come on, be plain about it for these good gentlemen, or stop wasting our time with your screeching!"

The woman's face turned pale at first, but blood and rage soon filled her back up again. "I'm sure I'll not say in polite company," she replied, glancing at the other two as though to convey some silent truth, "but we all know well why you'll never be married, Mairead Meur!"

She had stepped away from the wall before she realized she'd moved; hands knotted at her sides, sharp heels clacking on the stones. "Say it," she growled, "Say it or swallow it! I'll not stand here and be called nothing at all because you can't face the truth of your brother that all Ramphollow knows!"

Cait's mouth worked behind her tight pressed lips, her hands flexed at her sides, and for a moment, Mairead wondered if she would catch up a knife from the sideboard and come on. She had not yet decided whether she would raise a hand to stop it or not when Cait found the words she clearly wanted. "Oh, and I'll tell you what all Ramphollow knows, you unnatural creature—"

"That's enough." Elliot Crimmon came up close behind his wife, his one good hand bearing down heavy on her shoulder in case she'd not heard him rumble. Cait tried to turn on him, her eyes starting with outrage, but he gave her no chance. "This is a wedding, woman, not a brawling ring, and I'll not have my wife making a spectacle out of young Emily's day. You'll take yourself off home now if you can't keep a civil tongue in your head."

"I, keep a civil tongue!" Cait cried.

"Aye, you," Elliot said. "Get on now, and calm yourself down." He gave her a push that carried her halfway to the door. "I'll be out to join you in a moment or two," he called when the woman caught her feet, straightened up, and turned to him with the promise of revenge shining in her eyes. There was a hush in the long room. Someone tittered. Then, with a furious dignity, Cait Crimmon turned her back on the staring wedding guests and marched out of the house.

The roar of voices arose once again in her wake, and over it, Talin Embry gave a low whistle. "I've always said you're a brave man, Crimmon," he said.

Elliot waved off the praise. "Eh. It's high time someone took her in hand about that brother of hers," he said. "I'll give the lad house room at the inn on account of he's blood kin to Cait. And bless the woman, I do love her, but she's as much a fool over the boy as her mother was."

"All the same," Dr. Kerrow replied, "You'll have a few hard nights of that one."

To which the innkeeper only shrugged, and turned his attention to Mairead, who squared her shoulders to meet it. "Miss Meur." He nodded, respectful as if he'd passed her in the church on Sunday. "I'm sorry to hear that Our Durn's been troubling you and your good father. I've warned him off myself, for I know how he can be—me more than any, as he's under my own roof."

Mairead felt herself blushing at the courtesy. She'd never considered what it must be like for Elliot to live so long with his shiftless brother-in-law, who was surely just the sort to filch from home as readily as he did from anywhere else.

"I've told him," he went on before she'd found any words, "and I'll tell you: mischief and laziness is one thing, but this disgrace takes it a bridge too far. I'll not stand for it. If he gives you any more trouble, you let me know and I'll have a quick end to it. You'll see."

"Thank you, Mr. Crimmon," she managed at last, clenching tight against the urge to squirm away from his earnest regard. Not for her story against Durn—he'd gone to the holm with rape in mind, and if he hadn't tried it on her, well still he tried it. No, what unnerved her now, was the notion of Helzie, in her name, setting this good man against the wife he loved. And with the inn and its tavern square at Ramphollow's heart, who in the town would not suffer from such a war as that?

But if he sensed her distress, Elliot gave no sign. Instead, he nodded his goodnight to the two men, and headed for the door, where his wife might, or might not, be waiting for him to walk her back home.

Dr. Kerrow watched him go, then turned to regard Mairead. "You really ought to have come to see me at once, Miss Meur," he said, a blurry professionalism failing to stick to his face, "you might have been badly injured and not even realized it. These things can develop, you know."

And at that, she could no longer suppress the shudder. "It was a knock or two, nothing more," she answered, hoisting one of the tavern casks and hugging it to her chest. "I've had worse helping out at shearing time."

"But didn't he..." Talin began, then clammed up tight when good sense made its way through the whiskey.

"He tried," she said, "I never said he managed. Now excuse me please, I must get this to the barn. The musicians will be thirsty by now." And she fled to the back door before either of them could say another word.

The sky outside was dusted with clouds, still pink with the memory of day. The moon hung high already, a half circle on its way to black, just waiting for full dark to silver the fields and hills with her waning regard. A fitting sky for a wedding night, serenely unaware of the storm rolling over the sea. The weather report said it would be a fierce one, and would likely overrun the islands in a day or two, but you couldn't tell to look aloft now.

"Amazing." A voice beside her made her jump.

Mairead turned to find an officer, pale and narrow, holding up the wall beside the door through which she'd just come. "Pardon?" she said.

"Oh, I know you must be used to it, but for Heaven's sake, it's half ten, the sun's just got down and it's still nearly as bright as noon." He waved his cigarette at the arching sky. "How on earth do you Orcadians manage to sleep without any proper night at all?"

"Oh, same as you do it at home, I suppose." She found herself smiling at his petulant tone. "Only we get our nights in winter, whereas your London streetlights never do go out."

"Wiltshire," he corrected sourly. "Not so big on streetlights on the chalk downs. I'm Marcellus Putnam."

Mairead shifted her burden to shake the hand he thrust at her. "Well, Marcellus Putnam, if our long days trouble you so, I think you'll find that blackout curtains work both ways."

His eyebrows went up, but he laughed. "Clever. Where are you off to with that then?"

Mairead gave a nod at the open barn, bleeding golden light and drunken laughter across the yard. "Won't be much dancing if the fiddler goes dry."

"The fiddler?" Marcellus laughed. "He's soaked through already, I think. Ramsey's setting up the wireless in there now, so we'll have something we can dance to. We might as well bring that in though. Can't get the radio too drunk to play, can it?" He stepped away from the wall, reaching out toward her, but hesitated when she flinched away. "I can carry that for you," he said after an awkward moment. "It does look heavy."

It was on her tongue to snap that she could manage it well enough, and didn't need his help. But as he turned to the light, she could see how nervous he looked beneath his stiff-lipped reserve—how awkward and shy. He could hardly know anyone here, this man, not much more than a reedy boy from Wiltshire, with good breeding perched on him like a powdered wig. How lost he must feel here on the islands, surrounded by plain, sturdy crofters and fishermen who'd care nothing at all for the rank he'd been raised to.

A burst of music, tinny and quick, rolled out of the barn, followed by a cheer. *It's a dance*, she reminded herself sternly, *not an engagement*. Then she handed the cask to the stray Wiltshire boy, and conjured a smile. "Thanks. I'm Mairead."

"Mairead," he repeated, very nearly hiding his relief as he bumped out an elbow toward her. "Shall we go on in then?"

His smile when she made herself take his sleeve was nearly blinding.

As Aunt Jenn had predicted, once the officers saw that Mairead could manage the bold, modern dances they knew, they didn't let her sit down for a single one. Emily Braeson—no wait, it was Willet now—watched with mute fury from the chairs by the radio. Her sisters and friends made a show of staring and whispering their disapproval, but Mairead made a show of not caring one tiny bit.

Amy Bragg came over to try it on at one point, snidely butting in to ask Mairead to dance with her. It was an offer she clearly did not expect to make good on however, for she gasped and struggled when Mairead caught her hand and whirled her out onto the floor, to the cheers and applause of all the sailors. Mairead managed to take the girl twice around the room in a dizzying slipjig before she could yank herself loose and flee.

Unsurprisingly, it was Marcellus Putnam who stepped into Amy's place to finish the jig. Marcie, as the other officers called him, turned out to be one of the better dancers among them, though not so quick as Deen, so clever as Jean, nor so strong on the lifts as Tam. With him as a frequent partner, Mairead managed not to give herself any time to feel shy, or to wonder what all these strangers must think of her, or to think of anything except whatever steps her partner meant to take on next.

It couldn't last, of course. Eventually, the dance program on the wireless wound down, leaving Mairead to face a slow, dozy love song in the arms of a burly Yorkshireman whose name she hadn't been told. The lazy music gave her no shelter from the man's hopeful flirting, no way to hide her rising anxiety as he tried to chat her up. Where did she live that he'd not met her in town? Who taught her to dance? What did her friends call her? Why had he never seen her at the monthly parties on the base?

This is why! she wanted to shout. *Because it can't ever be just about the dancing! It's that I want, not you or your mates!* Mairead could feel her muscles, warmed from the exercise, tightening under his casual hands as she fought to get other, milder words out past the truth in her throat.

"Here now, what's wrong, sunbeam?" he asked her, only half concerned as she shivered, "you getting a cramp?"

"I wonder if you'd let me cut in please?" said a voice in kind, Irish tones. Turning their square, the Yorkshireman found Father Brian behind them, handsome and smart in his formal cassock. "It's just it's nearly time I left for the evening, and I'd like to have a word with Miss Meur before I do, Corporal Grundy."

He mightn't have been happy about yielding his dance to the young priest, as newly appointed to Ramphollow as any of the sailors, but Grundy did it all the same. Mairead held her breath as Father Brian settled their arms at a respectful distance, lest she weep with relief.

"Forgive me, dear, it's just you looked a bit distressed there." He smiled knowingly at Mairead's nonchalant shrug. Neither of them was fooled. "Well, anyway I didn't want to leave without speaking with you. I've been worried about you, you know, after our talk last Sunday week. Especially when you didn't come down last Sunday at all." Surprised, Mairead missed a step, but Father Brian covered it smoothly. "You see, it's important to me that you know I meant no disrespect by my suggestion, and most definitely that I had no improper intentions in it. I made it thinking only that you might simply be happier there."

Startled at last from her silence Mairead shook her head. "No, truly Father. I know you meant me only well by it. It's just… well, with Da as he is these days, I can't always get away. Not even for Mass."

"Yes, and I worry about that as well," he said, turning them smartly as they drew too near the chairs and the young folk resting upon them. "I do not approve of idle gossip, but in such a small town as Ramphollow, it's all but unavoidable. People talk, to me and around me, and I know your father will not be long for this world, Mairead."

She blinked hard, and choked back the pointless urge to protest the truth as false. Father Brian smiled, warm and sad, and went on breaking her heart. "Also, I know that most of the village is caught up in wondering where the next Keeper for the Selkeness Light will be hired from when he's gone."

"I've—" Mairead began.

"You've been keeping the light and the horn for a year now," he cut her gently off, "but in the eyes of the Crown, it's still a man's job, and a desperately important one with the Scapa Flow such a prime military target. And so, until he dies, the Crown will believe it's Mansie Meur who's keeping the tower alight.

"You will have to think of a future for yourself soon, Mairead, and the one I suggested is not so very bad, as futures go."

He turned them again, gave her a silent moment to gather herself as the Dorsey Brothers gave way to Glenn Miller. "But," she managed at last, "a convent? Me?" She shook her head. "I mean no disrespect, Father, it's just I've always thought that Sisters had to be more... well..." She struggled in vain for the word she wanted. "I've never felt the draw to a convent life. Not even once. And wouldn't God only want the most faithful sorts of women for His brides?"

He was silent for a long moment, his face calm and sad as they waltzed a square again and again. "The Almighty knows this world of ours is not perfect," he said at last, with the air of a potent truth that wanted careful saying. "And likewise, He knows there's some of His children who have no other place to fit into it than underneath His wing.

"Now it's true, He demands a greater measure of love and devotion from His chosen daughters and sons than from those who take easier roads," and here, he tipped a nod to Emily Willet, who'd taken advantage of the slower song to command her bridegroom's arm on the dance floor. "But for some of His children, the Church provides the best measure of peace and security they can hope for in this flawed world. Sanctuary, if you will," he smiled at her, "only for a lifetime."

She could see how it might be exactly so, but still the thought of kneeling in the church, and bending her shoulder to those towering vows made her want nothing more than to run. But she didn't know where she might run to, if she did. "It feels... sacrilegious in a way," Mairead said.

"You're thinking Old Testament, Miss Meur," the young priest chuckled, breaking their square to lead her from the dance floor as the waltz gave way to a faster number. "This is the God who so loved the world that He would sacrifice His only begotten son for its benefit," he said, turning to face her again where the barn doors opened wide onto the night. "This is the God who made you, just as you are; who knows everything about you, and who still thinks you're worthy of salvation. Can you really think He doesn't understand what you feel?" He patted her arm, and slipped it loose from his own. "Think about it, Miss Meur, and seriously this time. Promise?"

What could she do but nod? After all, he was right; she must find some future for herself somewhere, and was a convent life truly the worst of her very few choices?

"Pardon me, Father, Miss Meur," a man said from behind—an officer, young and smart as all the rest. "I wonder if I might have this dance with the young lady?" Father Brian tipped her a smile, knowing and a little sad, as he left her side and faded across the threshold of the night without any further advice.

"It's just a dance," she murmured to herself, watching him go. Then the young man coughed for her attention, and with a sigh, Mairead let herself be led back to the floor, and the ringing wall of music and motion too quick and wild to allow any thought to leak through.

After two dances though, she had to admit her heart was no longer in it. Crying off in the name of her new shoes, Mairead refused the next invitation, and slipped off to find Corporal Bonham, who hadn't stayed long in the dancing barn once the fiddler retired. She found him in the ring of chairs that had grown up around the old menye singers, who were dueling with folktales and rhymes at the fireside.

Walt Dennisson held the floor as she came in. "One spared to the sea is three spared to the land," he said, fixing the listeners by turns under his sharp gray stare. "And she made the children repeat it till they'd got it right. And then she told them, 'Run away home, bairns, and dunno pass the trink again—I came for once only!'"

Bonham looked back as Mairead slipped up behind his chair, but she lay a finger to her lips, and nodded his attention back to the storyteller before he could speak. Walt gave her a nod in return as he went on. "Well, when those children looked back from the foreshore, the tide was pouring through the trink and the water was high over the rocks. And do you think they could see any trace of those gray-cloaked women?

"Why no, none at all. But there were two fine, fat seals a-swimming off towards the point of Elseness. And that was the Selkie Woman's debt, repaid thrice over. That was the Seal's own honor."

Corporal Bonham pushed back his chair then, as the smattering of applause marked the old story's end. "Is everything all right, Miss Meur?" he asked, following her away from the gathered chairs. "You look a little pale."

"I'm fine," she lied, chafing her arms despite herself, "just a little tired, is all."

"Shall I drive you home then?"

She searched his face, relieved to find no leering shadow under his freckles, then she nodded. "Yes. Please."

The jeep handled the coast road better than Mansie's old truck ever had done, and quicker too. The moon still hung well over the horizon, lighting the road's turns and swells well out of the headlamps' reach, making the dodging of rocks, ruts, and stray sheep that much easier. Corporal Bonham was content to let them ride in silence, after Mairead failed to make good on his attempts at small talk. Whether he believed her claims of fatigue or not, he was at least a good sport about it.

"Take the fork just here," she called to him at last, holding on as he slid them around the corner faster than she'd have dared. Ahead the Selkeness light painted the ridgeline in black relief over and over again. Seeing that old familiar flash pattern that meant home, Mairead felt something inside her uncurl at last.

"I can't imagine living out here," Bonham said over the wind, "so far from everything. So quiet... and look at all those stars. You must love it."

Mairead glanced at him, surprised, then nodded. "I do. Raised to it, I suppose. See up ahead there, where the road curves up toward the headland?" He nodded, following her point. "Well, just before it is the road down to the lighthouse. You can let me off up at the top."

"Oh, I don't mind driving you—"

"You will mind, once you've to back this jeep up the slope to get her out again," Mairead cut him off. "There's no place below to turn her around, you see, and no one to haul you out of the ditch till morning, if you should get her stuck. I'd rather walk down, truly."

He pulled up alongside the narrow drive, and peered down it as though considering his chances. Mairead used the moment to swing herself out of the jeep.

"Here now," he called as she started off round the back, "at least take this torch." He briefly rummaged in the back before handing her the cylinder of metal and glass. "That way I can watch to make sure you get down all right without turning an ankle. Those are no shoes for a trek like that in the dark."

"Well, that's truth," she admitted, and switched it on.

"Besides, you can bring it back to me at next month's dance down the base." He grinned when Mairead rolled her eyes. "The lads will give me no peace about you till they hear you'll come, you know. So do try and find a little mercy in you for a poor sailor far from home, won't you?"

"I'll try," said Mairead, and turned her back on him to begin her long descent.

Once she reached the shed, she turned back and waved the torch over her head. Up on the road, the jeep's headlamps flickered off, then back on again, and its engine rattled it back into motion. She watched the twin gleams rake across the night as it turned, and then only its red tail showed through the dust as Bonham drove off.

"Right then," she murmured, and turned toward the house. The torchlight caught a metal gleam down by the beach, and Mairead groaned to recall the mortar and tools she'd meant to get cleared away before the wedding, all still sitting beside the shingle wall. With the storm on its way, she hardly knew when she'd be able to finish the work, and her tools oughtn't to weather any more neglect either. She'd been lucky the islands had had little worse than fog in the week she'd left them out unheeded, but now such luck was done.

Mairead had long since fallen entirely out of love with the shiny new dancing shoes, but she didn't much like the idea of having to come back out again once she'd gone in to change. Nor of venturing down to the shingle with nothing on her feet but her aunt's stockings. So she tucked the torch under her arm and went to collect the bucket as she was.

She got it in hand, held well away from the new dress, and shined the light back up toward the house. Then she saw just a flicker of movement before a great pain blossomed over the back of her skull and scattered her thoughts across the shingle with a roar.

"Where is it?"

She blinked, took a breath. The bucket of tools had rolled down to the waterline, where the foamy waves were rolling it back and forth like a child's toy. Somewhere a sea bird creeled, high and lonely.

"Damn you, where did you hide it?" Something hooked hard under her shoulder, and the beach lurched aside for the sky until Durn Helzie put his face in the way.

She worked her jaw, spitting gravel, or maybe teeth until she could mumble, "Wha?"

Helzie's face twisted the harder in the electric torch's light, and the world lurched again as he caught her dress to shake her upright. "Don't you be coy with me, or I'll bash you again! You tell me where it is, or I'll..." He brandished the cudgel against the moonlit sky.

He still thought she had the skin, she realized muzzily, grasping weakly at the hand gripping her collar, but she couldn't give him what was gone.

"Don't you lie to me!" Helzie screamed. Had she spoken that aloud?

"Gave it back," she added, just in case she had. "A week ago. The selkie has it—aow!" He backhanded her, the cudgel making his fist heavy enough to strike sparks behind her eyes.

"I said don't lie!" With a great wrench, Durn hauled her to her feet, giving her a shove when she would have toppled again. "You think you're clever, but I have your measure, and I'll not be robbed by the likes of you. You'll show me where it is."

"Or else what?" Mairead asked him, her wits enough recovered to let him shove her toward the house without fighting. "You'll kill me over a bride who doesn't want you anyway?" She staggered away from another shove, but managed to keep her feet. "The law doesn't overlook murdering just because there's a war on, you idiot."

"Oh, it won't take murdering," Helzie leered, pushing her up the stairs to the lighthouse's front door. Without the skin to hide, she hadn't locked it when they'd gone out, and though Aunt Jenn had left the light on above it, she'd never think to lock the door. Helzie pushed his cudgel against Mairead's neck until she opened it all the same.

"You'll show me where it is," he said, shoving her forward again as the door swung away, "and never you mind what I want it for."

She stumbled in the dark room, cursed as she barked her shins, and had suddenly quite enough. She whirled on her heel, caught Helzie's arm before the club could swing again, and shoved him into the doorframe with a growl. "You'll get nothing here, you bully," she told him, twisting hard on his wrist until he let the cudgel drop, and using all her weight to pin the man where he stood. "What you want is gone back to the sea, and I'll not have the likes of you in my home regardless!"

He went still beneath her weight, something jagged and ugly flashing through his glare.

"You... you really gave it back?" he asked, breath thick with whiskey.

"Course I did, you tit," Mairead replied. "First chance I could! I could no more keep a Seal Bride here than you could in the attic over your sister's pub!" In the second it took for her to roll her eyes in disgust, Helzie struck, bashing the ridge of his forehead square into her nose.

Mairead reeled back, cracked her bruised head against the doorframe when he shoved, and then slithered to the floor. Caught in the whelming rush of a great black undertow, she couldn't so much as twitch when he stepped over her sprawled legs, then used one of them to haul her over the threshold. Any thought she might have taken to fight further ended when the door clipped her temple as she slid past.

When at last the roaring eased, Mairead found herself in the kitchen, feet bound up to her hands behind her, and the both lashed down to the cooker's great iron leg. Helzie sat cross legged on the floor beside her, flipping through one of the family albums with a cigarette in one hand, and one of Da's good whiskey glasses at his knee. She'd have bitten him, had he only been close enough.

She was working up the means to spit at the bastard when he noticed the state of her, and proffered a grin. "Not only are you an unnatural bitch, Mairead Meur, it turns out you're a liar as well."

"Bollocks," she coughed, her bloody cheek sticking to the cold tiles.

"Oh, it's no good carrying on," he waved his finger in her face, the smoke following to clog her throat with loathing. "She's been here. I've seen her here, lurking about the place when she thought no one could see. Now why would a selkie be following the likes of you about on dry land if she didn't have to stay?"

Mairead groaned, letting her eyes close in weary disgust. "I don't know. I don't care. She took it, and she went. That's all."

Helzie snapped the album shut with a bang, and slung it aside. "Now let's have no more of that," he leered, catching down a dishrag from the counter and stooping to shove it past her lips despite her very best efforts to bite him. "If you can't be truthful, you'd best be properly silent for once in your life, and let me search it out myself. I daresay there can't be many places you'd have hidden the thing around here…"

"Mairey?" Her father's voice drifted from above, wary and tremulous. Helzie turned after the sound like a dog on point. "Mairey, who's that with you down there? Who're you talking to?"

Da, no! But all that made it past the rank wad of cloth was a shrill sort of moan. She thrashed against the knots, inasmuch as she could, rutching the skirt high under her hip and smearing the bodice on the bloody tiles, but getting no slack for her efforts. Helzie toed her ribs and stood laughing while she coughed the pain through.

"Well then, this'll make the searching easier, won't it?" he said, tossing back the whiskey. "The Old Man'll know where you've laid it by, I'll warrant, and he'll know better than to keep it back once I make things clear to him as well."

He would, too, Mairead realized with a sick twist in her belly; all his life, Mansie Meur had done whatever he could to see his children safe, his daughter safest of all. Let Helzie only threaten to harm her in his sight, and her father would kill himself to save her. Even if it would not save her at all. But she could gain no leverage, no measure of freedom to stop the murderous bastard as he dusted his hands together and headed for the stairs, calling, "Hello, Mr. Meur, it's me, Durn Helzie, remember? I played rugger with your man Deen at school?"

"My Deen's not here," came the reply, closer now, as though her father had climbed out of bed to answer. "He's gone away to the war. What are you wanting with us?" Both relieved and horrified at the chill in the old man's voice, Mairead redoubled her fight against Helzie's damned knots.

"Oh, I know it, sir. Only, see, he'd borrowed something of mine before he went," despite the strain of blood in her ears, Mairead heard the lie fall flat, "and I'm needing it again now. Perhaps you've seen it? It's... It's an old furry coat. Belonged to me mum years back, and now me sister's taken a fancy to—"

"You stop there, thief!" Mairead stilled, shocked to hear the steel that had been missing from her father's voice so long.

Helzie, it seemed, did not note it at all. "I wondered if Deen hadn't given it to your Mairead before he went away? It's a little thing a girl might fancy, but my sister's got a right to what's hers, after all, and—"

"I said you're to stop!" A sound of metal on metal, gears gnashing their teeth, brass shoved into a chute of steel as the breech snapped closed around it. Mairead would have shouted if she could.

She'd hid his old service rifle down in the cellar with the tools months ago! When—and how—had Da managed to get past her to find it?

"Mr. Meur, there's no call for that." Helzie's tread no longer sounded the creaky stairs, but his wheedling tone took up a wary note. "You'll give yourself a turn if you don't calm down. Why not set that old gun aside now, before someone gets—"

"I know what it is you're wanting, young liar, and you cannot have it!" her father spat—from the hallway? Or had he come to meet Helzie at the head of the stairs? Was he shaking behind the rifle's rust-spotted muzzle? Perhaps leaning one shoulder into the wall just so he could stand? The fool. The mad old fool! Mairead's breath hitched, helpless in her clogged throat as her father drove home his point by cocking the hammer back. "Now get you gone from our home before I put shot to your arse!"

There was a long silence. A creak of weight shifting on the middle stair. Then Durn Helzie laughed. "So you do have it. I knew the bitch was lying."

"You get—"

"Oh, aye, I'm leaving all right," Helzie laughed. "But now I know the skin is here, I can come back for it whenever I like. And neither you, nor her downstairs, nor that rusty old gun will keep me from what's—"

The shotgun eclipsed his words with thunder and the sound of a great, loose weight tumbling down uneven stairs. Mairead could just see the landing from where she lay, could just see Helzie's arm reaching out into open air, flexing weakly before it went limp and still.

"Da?" She moaned around the rag, voice cracking. Again, louder when the old man made no answer. Breath whistling through her nose, she struggled not to cry, to slow her charging heart, to quiet the blood pounding in her ears, so she could listen.

Then at last, a scraping, shuffling noise brought her hope once more. A groan. A cough that rattled and wheezed. Mairead held her breath, praying. A rustle of cloth on cloth. Scraping, as of nails on polished wood. A whimper. A sob. A clumsy thud of boots on the stairs.

Boots. She closed her eyes. Boots, not the bare feet of a bed-ridden old man.

Mairead bit at the old rag with all her will as Durn Helzie came slumping down the stairs, one hand clapped fast to his shoulder, bit it lest she scream, and draw his notice once more. His dirty boots dragging, Helzie rattled off of the sofa and toppled the end table, where stood the only lamp in the room. It shattered at his feet, and night reclaimed the house.

There he hung for a moment, little more than a hulking shape against the porch light's secondhand glow, his panting breath the loudest sound in the whole house. Then he whimpered again, breathed a curse, and staggered to the front door, where at last he let his wound go to fumble for the knob. If he heard Mairead's gasp as the porch light shone across his shirtsleeve, scarlet from shoulder to cuff, Helzie gave no sign of it.

Instead, he tumbled down the steps with a grunt and a rattling thud, smashing the porch light down with a flailing arm as he fell. The door banged idly behind him. Then, after a long moment, Mairead heard the gravel of the walk sliding as he got up and slouched off across the night.

And no matter how Mairead shouted into the reeking silence that followed his retreat, she could not coax it to break.

Eventually, she slept. It was understandable, of course. There was only so much pain, frustration, and helplessness anyone could take without some surcease. Her head ached, her neck cramped at the effort of spitting out the rag, her legs and hands went numb in their scratchy nooses. The dark house went cold around her, the great lit tower above it and the churning engine below the only signs of life. The reserve tank of fuel could keep the light turning well into the next day on any normal night, but only if someone switched the feed before the primary tank ran dry. Which it would do sooner than normal, as they'd lit the great lamp early, and left it flashing into the afternoon when they'd all gone down to Ramphollow's church. The light could fail any time. Any time.

Surely someone would come to see about that. Someone down in Ramphollow, or off its shoreline, someone not yet blind drunk from the wedding would fret for want of that white beam scraping the darkness. Perhaps a miraculously sober fisherman would find himself concerned that the horn did not sound when the morning fog rolled in thick off the sea. Surely, surely someone would come out to see what was wrong at Selkeness point, and they'd find Mairead here, trussed out like a culled lamb and lashed to the stove.

The blood on her cheek dried and cracked, wet only by what furious tears she could not manage to quell. The wind tapped the door back and forth like a child bored with his toy. The light swept the sky again, and again, and again.

No one came to find her. No sound of movement from above reassured her that her father had only knocked himself down with that damned gun. Winded himself, most likely. Slept where he'd fallen, or wakened in confusion and taken himself quietly back to his bed while Mairead lay dazed. Mansie was nearly deaf, and the rest of him barking, and that was why he would not answer her calls. Heaven grant that he'd not taken it into his head to slip past her in the dark, and follow the intruder from his home.

And Helzie... He might return at any time, as mad as before, but most likely better armed. If he could steal a boat from his neighbors, he could steal a gun from some sailor in the pub. Remembering the vicious light in his eyes, Mairead knew he'd not think twice on coming back with it to kill them both.

So Mairead applied her wits to working loose his knots, and when the rope proved tougher than her bloodless fingers, to sawing the cord back and forth against the stove's rough iron leg until she could move no more without a rest. And in the grip of that rest, without meaning to at all, she slept.

It was a fractious, shivering thing, cracked through with bad dreams, panicked waking shouts, and a few angry tears. She could not tell what time had passed in silence, and though she could feel the creeping damp of sea mist upon her skin, she could not judge the weight of the fog from inside the solid night.

Shivering overtook her, for the tiles were cold, the torn and bloodied party dress a fragile little thing. And, too, her head was still full of unwary ships breaking their hearts on the rocks and slipping under the waves with groans of despair when the Selkeness light burned itself out and left the coastline dark to the coming storm.

"Damn you," she choked out to drown the noise in her head, "I will get loose. I will!" Mairead gathered herself to work the ropes again, fighting a brief war against the agony of shoulders and knees to make herself move at all. Then bellowed in shock when the fibers gave way with a lurch and a sudden shredding noise. She screamed again as her legs and arms flopped free, the release waking every inch of her to cramping agony. Mairead retched against the gripping pain, unable to breathe as blood filled her cold limbs with fire and pins. She hardly noticed the soft tread beside her until hands came brushing her hair from her face, and a voice shushed her, low and musical in the dark.

"Hurts," she managed, pressing her face into the softness that gathered her close. "It hurts!"

"Breathe to it," the voice answered, and strong fingers worked a cold, sharp spell against the knots around her swollen wrists. A moment later, her feet came free of each other, and Mairead could flop over onto her back at last, gasping as the pain roared over her like a tide.

When next she was aware of anything, Mairead found herself in her bed, watching the dark-eyed girl wind her wrist in clean white strips. The window behind her stood open to the night, the wind bearing in the scent and sound of the tide in a flutter of dimity curtains. How had she come to be upstairs? Surely the selkie girl was much too slight to have carried her.

"You are not so heavy as that," the girl replied with a little smile as the dark sky swept to one second of brilliance and back again, sketching a brief, bright halo around her head. The lace collar of Mairead's Sunday dress blazed in that second, like window frost against the dark tumble of the girl's hair.

"Da's seen to the light?" Mairead asked, for want of anything cleverer to say.

The girl glanced at the door, and her little smile dimmed. "No," she said, making a neat knot at Mairead's wrist, and biting off the remnant so her breath along Mairead's arm made her shiver. "He wasn't up to it, so I did." Mairead's shock must have shown on her face, for the smile came back again, this time with a sly glint to boot. "It wasn't that hard—it has got a switch, after all."

"But it's not that simple! You've got to fill both of fuel reservoirs, and—" She trailed off as a broad, soft hand pressed her gently but inexorably back into the pillows.

"I know," the seal girl said, serious now, "I watched you do it so I'd get it all right. The fog's blown off for now, so until the storm comes on, I've left the horn go, but all the rest is done. You can rest now, truly."

But Mairead hadn't made it past... "You... you watched me?" She nodded. "Then Helzie wasn't lying—"

The girl cocked her head. "Helzie?"

"The one who..." Mairead waved her bandaged hand vaguely in the direction of the holm, then felt her stomach clench tight remembering. "He'll come back. He said he'd come back again!" She caught at the girl's hands. "You mustn't let him catch you!"

"Hush now," the girl pressed her back down again, and flashed a grin full of neatly pointed teeth. "You let me worry about the thief, eh? Once-caught, he'll not find me such easy prey as all that. Nor you neither, now I'm here." Then she freed her hand with a deft twist and turned to the night table, taking up a bowl and plate. "Are you hungry?"

It was on Mairead's tongue to say she wasn't, but then the smell reached her and her stomach rowled awake. The girl grinned her pointed grin, and allowed Mairead to struggle upright before handing the bowl and spoon over. As before, the stew was a mélange of fish, mussels, potatoes, and herbs, both alike, and different to the pottage they'd been living on the week before.

The girl watched Mairead eat for a moment. "There's bread as well," she said, setting the plate and a brown loaf that had definitely not been in the house that morning beside Mairead's hip.

"You bake?" was all she could think to say.

The answering smile was coy and gleaming. "I do many things." At which Mairead could only flush guiltily, and break herself off a piece.

When the bowl was empty, the girl took it back, helped Mairead to recline again, and then reached to set her brothers' photo onto the bed beside her pillow. "I noticed you're fond of this," she said in answer to Mairead's confusion, and tipped a nod toward her brothers' smiling faces.

"The tall one's Tam," Mairead found herself saying. "He's the oldest of us by five years. Deen and Jean came two years later, and then in three years, me. Our mum died just after, so we're the lot."

"And where were they, these brothers of yours, when the thief came here with murder in his heart?"

The trace of scorn brought Mairead's back up bristling. "There's a war on, and someone must keep the Hun from overrunning us all. The Meur men are not too good to do their duty like the rest!" The girl's flinch checked her, and she tempered her ire before going on. After all, what would a seal know about warfare? "They're sailors in the Queen's navy," she said, pointing to the jaunty caps all three wore in their photos.

"Sailors," mused the girl, stealing a glance at Mairead before turning back to examine the photo. "Handsome."

Mairead smiled to see the seal girl's finger trace the curve of Tam's cheek. They were handsome, and roguish all three, they knew it. "They're the beauties of the family," she allowed fondly. "Not a girl on these islands they couldn't have if they'd but crooked a finger."

The seal girl tilted her head a moment, gazing at Mairead with not quite half a smile. Then she leaned close, and under pretext of settling the covers, put her mouth close against Mairead's hair to murmur, "They couldn't have me. But you, now..."

And then the seal girl kissed her. Soundly. Sweetly. One palm pressed over Mairead's charging heart to moor her down in pillows and heat lest that kiss sweep her entirely away. One of them made a desperate, hungry sound, equal kin to sob and sigh, and with a single, shocked wriggle the kiss fitted itself snug and solid between them. No room for words, for shame, for a lick of care that anyone might come and see, and watch Mairead drowning in arms and eyes and a rain of dark hair far softer than any fur pelt...

She thought of air only when the girl took her mouth away again. Even though the blood roared in her ears for want of it, Mairead almost forgot to breathe even then, distracted by the blaze in those endless eyes. A gentle hand stroked her hair from her face, and the lips that had so possessed her curved in a smile very nearly as wicked. "You have a rest now. I'll just go and finish the washing up."

"But—" Mairead caught at the girl's hand, but it slipped like water from her grasp. Then she was dancing out the door and away, her long legs flashing in the swirl of Mairead's Sunday dress, and there was nothing for it but to lay back and wonder.

Which is where sleep found her, not a minute later.

The rumble of distant thunder wakened her from dreams of blue and green. For a moment, still dream-witched, Mairead thought of drowning and panicked. But then the great light sliced through the dank, chill air, the storm-horn yowling after: the lullaby she'd known all her life long. She let go her aching breath in a long sigh beneath its bellow, and waited, blinking, for her racing heart to ease.

A weight against her back shifted. A voice murmured damply, wordlessly against her shoulder. The seal girl reached over Mairead's waist, pressing close with pillowy breasts as she slid her fingers down to where Mairead's hand tangled in the curls of her own loins.

Mortified to be so caught out, Mairead felt her face blaze hot in the darkness. She jerked her hand away, but could not suppress a torn gasp as her fingertips scraped roughly, wetly, through her sex.

"Shhh," the seal girl said, tangling their fingers together and gently, inexorably pressing Mairead's hand back to where it had been, "you needn't stop for my sake." Her lips were a molten graze along Mairead's neck, chilling when the wind gusted in through the open window to prickle fine hairs erect and nipples straining tight.

She shivered, her hand unsure below her belly, neither shield-stiff, nor yet limp and useless where it pressed against her sex. "I was asleep, I didn't mean to—" A finger pressed through her own, sought and found a gasp smothered in Mairead's slick folds. Underneath her helpless groan, Mairead was sure she heard the seal girl chuckle.

"'Tis better done waking, you know," she said, tangling their feet and drawing one of Mairead's backward to give her fingers room to explore. She placed a kiss on Mairead's shoulder, then another below it, and another, the little stiff points of her breasts like teasing heralds to where her mouth would surely follow. Too shaken to speak, Mairead let the girl keep her hand imprisoned, fingers twined wet and writhing until the slow parade of kisses crowned the point of her hip, and she heard the seal girl murmur, "Roll back..."

And she did, the fingers of her free hand reaching wildly for her pillow, the better to smother her rising urge to wail aloud. But her fingers tangled not in linen, but in soft leather and thick, short fur. Then she did cry out, jerked free of questing lips and fingers, and might have fallen out of the bed entirely, if not for the girl's weight across her knees. She tugged at the pelt with both hands, rolled the both of them about until she could haul it out from under her.

"No! Oh no," she cried, pushing it at the girl, rumpled and musky and lovely where she sprawled at the foot of Mairead's bed, "I gave it back to you! I never meant to keep it!"

"I know," the girl answered, and her voice was unaccountably sad. "I wouldn't bring it back knowing you didn't want it." Then she slipped from the bed and padded around the side without a thought for her nakedness as she struck a match and touched the little kerosene lamp awake with it. "That one's not mine though. Here, look," she plucked up the mask from where it dangled against Mairead's elbow, and turned it to the light. "It's much too dark overall, and my face has not this cast of gold where yours does."

"Where mine—" Mairead gulped. "What do you mean? I've never seen this pelt. It's certainly not mine."

The girl shook the match to death with an angry snap of her wrist, and flung its twisted corpse neatly out the window. "Well, it's not His either, and that's for sure," she said with a nod toward Da's room at the end of the hallway. "Even were it a bull's hide, which it isn't, no Seal-Kin would keep his own pelt wadded at the bottom of a wardrobe. The mice and spiders nesting in it had better claim than him," Then she reached out to smooth Mairead's hair, pillow-knotted and awkward in her eyes, and her fingers slipped from the gold to the brown, thick fur without pause. "And you've a better claim to it than anyone living, I think."

Mairead gasped, shivered at the touch as it wandered down the thick fall of the pelt where it draped over her shoulder, her breasts, her knotted fists until finally it pooled in her lap. The girl's fingers felt as warm and savage to her where they trailed dark paths through the seal fur as they had upon her own living skin. She felt the fine hairs of her back rise to it, felt a delicious shiver race prickling, tickling, wrongwise up one thigh, and coil hotly beneath her belly.

The girl scratched gently along one leathery flipper, and Mairead could not stop the reflexive jerk of her own foot.

"Oh," she breathed, and let herself be tipped back again as the seal girl climbed astride, the soft fur crushed and lush between them. Her hips bucked to feel the weight settle firmly around them, heat fierce and damp against her own. "Oh, it isn't yours…"

"No, it's not," the seal girl answered, nuzzling the pelt out of the way so she could kiss Mairead breathless again. "And so you cannot command me upon it. Not to stay, and not to go away again, either."

"Oh, dear God," Mairead groaned, tugging at the fur, suddenly eager to have it gone from between them, to feel the girl's skin and sweat and sex against her own, "why ever would I tell you to go away?"

"I had wondered that," the girl replied, lifting away obligingly, then pressing close again with all her weight and a kiss besides. "But so you did." At Mairead's confused look, she sat back and half shrugged, her own dark eyes carefully neutral. "When I came here to you at first, after the moon. You would not have me, and bade me go."

The new skin forgotten, Mairead thrust it at the wall so she could reach for the girl astride her. "I would not have you unwilling," she said, and her palms curled to the dip of the girl's waist as though they'd been carved to fit nowhere else. "I'd not have anyone who wanted to run, as you did, but I didn't say to go." The girl's closed look did not yield, and Mairead swallowed. "Did I?"

"Aye, you did," she said with a nod. But then she smiled, wicked and lovely, and leaned close to purr against Mairead's ear again, "But you never bade me stay away."

Mairead felt her fingers clutch soft skin, alarmed at the heated swipe of a tongue along the private, inner ridge of her ear. Heard her own cry, harsh and desperate before she could bite it back. Her da had to be asleep. Dear God, let him be asleep, for what would he say to walk in and find her tangled with this creature, this smooth, soft, lovely girl who tasted her like she was precious rare, who treasured her with hands never callused to a tool, who touched her as if she knew every one of Mairead's most secret, most desperate dreams.

"Wait!" She broke from the kiss with a drowning gasp, caught the girl's wrist to still it between her thighs. "Wait. It's just. Da's only down the hall, and I've..." she swallowed, fixed under the girl's fathomless gaze. "It's just I've never..."

The girl laughed, short and sharp, and not quiet in the least. "You have. I heard you t'other night."

And Mairead felt herself blush yet again. "No, I mean..." she leaned up, stole a kiss that was almost chaste, and whispered her damning confession, "never with... another. Another girl. I don't know what to do."

"I do," she said, and rolled Mairead onto her back with another of those kisses she felt in her toes, in her scalp, in her belly, and in her soul. A tug at her knees to splay them wide, and the girl flung a leg between them to pin Mairead down again, holding one of her ankles up high so that the heat between them met in a slick, crackling glide.

"Wait," Mairead heard herself bleat again. "Wait. I should. Will you?" She gulped, closed her eyes and forced herself to concentrate past the yowling need that coiled tight inside her sex. "Will you tell me your name? I don't even know your name."

The girl did not wait, but bore down and slid with a liquid roll of her hips. "Nor do I know yours," she growled, fretting back and forth along the cradle of Mairead's sex just as the tide might toy a pebble, "though I know your smell, and the feeling of your fingers sliding through my fur as you spend."

"Please tell me," Mairead gasped, urging her own hips into the dance as in the welter of softness, a hard, hungry bud clenched up tight as a fist, "I want to know how to remember you when you leave."

"So you can use it to summon me back?"

"No. Ah, sweet Jesus!" She clutched at the girl, a knee, a breast, anything she could hold as she tightened, as the need inside her began to ache and itch and claw for release. "Not unless you'd want to come."

The girl's teeth and eyes flashed, savage and lovely as she drove Mairead down again and again and again. "Oh, I'd want to," she said. "If I had your name, I'd summon you down below the storm. Keep you there till you forgot the feel of dust, and the smell of diesel smoke forever." Her thrusts became shorter, more breathless, more brutally accurate. A sweating flush bloomed across the girl's cheeks and rolling breasts as she panted, "If I had your name. Had your skin. I'd never. Let. You. Go!"

The threat crashed home in a roar of blood; the spiraling tension peaking needle-sharp and breathless before it burst into a whelming, tumbling roar that wound Mairead taut and shaking beneath the onslaught. Her sex pulsed, thrust, shied, and grasped for more, dear God, please more. She drowned aloud, with her mouth gulping salt air and musk, and her hands full of slick, sweaty skin. And still the seal girl did not stop, but rode Mairead on through her release, surging, rolling, grinding perilously close to real pain before she too fetched up, taut and thrashing, to pulse slick fire afresh between them.

Mairead caught her with both arms when she fell. She tucked the girl's neat, fine skull into the hollow of her shoulder, and held them both until the tremors eased. Breath slowed, sweat dried, the waves muttered absently through the drone of the tower's horn. Mairead was nearly asleep, and therefore could be forgiven her recklessness, because she positively did not intend, between one softening breath and the next, to murmur her name into the damp hollow of the seal girl's ear.

"Guessed it wrong." She felt the girl's pointed smile against her neck, and shook her head.

"No, it's mine. My name. My mother chose it after Da named the three boys."

"Ah." The girl purred, yielding to a stretch that pressed her greedily close again. "Naturally she did, Mairead of the Sea." Then in a sudden rustle of damp linens and sweaty skin parting, the girl rolled out of Mairead's arms and bed in one wriggle. "Come on," she said, turning to offer her hand.

"What? Come where?"

The girl flashed that sharp-toothed grin, and caught the brown pelt up from the night table. "Come along," she said, and thrust the pelt behind her, like a wicked child stealing another's mac, "the tide's low, and I want to go outside."

"But..." Mairead rolled from the bed herself, still shaking but unable to be left behind, "But Da. I can't leave him with a storm blowing in—"

"He sleeps, beloved; peaceful and deep." She took another step toward the door. "We'll be back long before he wakens. I want to show you something."

Mairead glanced at the open window, considering fog, rain, and the looming storm inbound over the North Sea. The dark sky did not yet show it, but she could feel the pressure dropping, and knew it had to be coming on. Still, "Show me what?"

The girl slung the brown pelt around her shoulders, then tied it off at the side like a Viking warrior's cape and toed up high to kiss Mairead with a wicked sort of grin, every inch of her a predator.

"I want to show you where I've hid my skin."

They walked to the holm by the twisting light of the beacon, their feet bare to the round-stoned shingle, their skins taut with drying sex and sweat, the seal girl in her borrowed skin, Mairead under the weighty drape of Da's old oilskin cape. Strangely, Mairead hardly felt the cold through the swinging cloth, though on any other such morning she'd have had to put on three shirts and a jumper just to keep from chattering chill. There was a strange, persistent heat along her chest and belly as she went, as though she could feel the warmth of the seal girl's shoulders and back against her. And though she knew she ought to be mortified to walk; so nearly naked along the shingle where anybody might come along and see, the truth was she couldn't bring herself to care.

Not with the seal girl's fingers twined tight with hers. Not with the memory of kisses so fierce she almost feared to end them still hovering about her lips. Not with the smell of what they'd done still haunting the back of Mairead's throat—a lush, decadent perfume that the freshening sea wind served only to enhance. Any shame she might have expected to feel now that her long-silenced yearnings had finally been met simply could not make their way through the press of warm, flustered amazement.

She had lain with this girl, this mad, wild, fey creature—had lain with her and loved her now enough to let herself be led nearly naked to the shallow trink, and the holm rising beyond it. How could she begin to worry about the sin of it now? The ghost of old Father Eames could not begin to shame her when Mairead didn't even know how to rank her sins in order. Woman with woman? Woman unwedded, surrendered to lust in heathen arms? Woman partaking of sexual pleasure at all, not merely enduring it for the child to come after? Or did the selkie not count as a woman at all in God's eyes? Would the sin be named as woman lying with a wild beast?

No. Mairead gave a defiant glance at the silvering horizon behind the headland, and decided that the brief summer night did not have room for sins in it. Sin and guilt and the coming storm could all wait for morning. She'd decide then whether she cared about any of it.

"Tide's turning," the girl said, striding into the trink, and leading Mairead along behind.

Gasping at the cold roll of seawater over her ankles, Mairead clutched the oilskin coat higher around her and pushed through the stream. "We'll have to hurry. Once it's come in, the trink's too deep to wade, and the river's too fast to swim." The girl flashed her a grin, impish and sly, over her freckled shoulder. Mairead blushed again. "Too fast for me to swim, anyhow."

"Well we'd best not linger then," she laughed, and dropping

Mairead's hand, ran along the trink, splashing wild, careless footprints into the onrushing tide. Sure beyond the telling, it seemed, that Mairead would follow wherever she led.

For good reason. Mairead was somewhat less sanguine about running full-tilt through the rising water, so the advantage of her longer legs and uninjured feet could not make up the seal girl's lead. She didn't catch up until they'd reached the shore, and clambered up to the wind-scored top, where once the whole clan of selkies had gathered. Where they had danced, fought, sported, and loved, and where Mairead had watched like a beggar through the tavern window.

At the promontory, they stopped; the very point, Mairead realized, where the girl had dived into the waves the first time she'd tried to return the skin. "Was it wise to hide it here?" she asked. "Helzie knew you'd been here before, and he—"

The girl stilled her lips with a finger and smiled. "That vicious creature's not worth another thought, beloved," she answered, cuddling up for a kiss. "I'll not share one scrap of your attention with the likes of him." Then she turned to the truss of ropes pegged along the stone brim, and knelt to select one among them.

"But those are my lobster pots." Even as Mairead said it, she knelt to help the girl haul it up from the sea, giving no second thought to losing whatever catch might be within.

"And quite a neat place to hide one's treasure they are, too," the girl replied as the wicker bundle bumped up into reach. The pelt inside was sodden, slick, and gray as slate. Constellations of freckles gleamed black in the predawn gloom as its owner pulled it across her lap to smooth out the salty water with practiced hands. Mairead knelt nearby, not quite daring to reach out and touch the gray pelt again, though her palms itched with its memory.

Out over the sea, the promised storm flashed and grumbled to itself, firefly specks lit the waves beneath them, and fishing boats raced to bring in their pre-dawn catches. Once her father and brothers would have been among them, the *Ursilla Meur* running low with cod and pollock, but fast enough still to lead the pack home to warm hearth, dry socks, and breakfast. Now the boat lay rotting in her berth, as idle and empty as the man who had owned her; as scattered as the boys who once had made her fly. As the thunder marched growling overhead, Mairead had to wonder if this would not be the storm to finally sink her.

"We knew you watched us," the seal girl's voice drew Mairead's attention back to land. "The whole clan did. We could smell you in the dark, could sometimes see the moon shining off your yellow hair when you'd peek out past the thrust. One or two of the bulls wanted to go and ask why you would not come join the dancing, but..." and here she did glance up, her gaze solemn and dark beneath the thick tumble of hair, "but we would not let them. We wanted you to come down on your own."

"I..." Her voice cracked.

I didn't know, didn't think I could, should, didn't dare to hope, couldn't begin to dream you would...

Taking a deep breath, she tried again. "I don't know how to dance. Not like you do."

With a smile that showed how little she believed it, the seal girl knelt up and pushed the oilskin off Mairead's shoulders. "Then I'll just have to show you the way of it," she said, and slung the wet gray fur around her back, ignoring Mairead's yelp and shudder as she deftly knotted it in place. "Up you get, then," the girl said, catching Mairead's hands and tugging.

It wasn't the same, this dancing; not with only two of them in the predawn gloom; not with the pelt dripping icy seawater along her back and legs; not with the clouds grumbling out over the North Sea, black where the coming dawn would paint them with scarlet menace. Mairead was all too aware of her soft, human feet and bony, awkward knees as they went; she felt all corners and edges, a poppet of sticks and rags for the Beltane blaze in the hands of a sweetly feral child who loved her just enough to burn her to the ground without a second thought.

Mairead did try her best though, gamely stumbling after her girl through patterns of tread and trip and whirl and weave that seemed half mad on the slick rocks above the crashing sea. Any moment, she was sure, she would turn an ankle and fall over the edge. Or the fishing boats would blow hither, and their lookouts train glass and brass along the headland to where the holm split the river, and see them there. Or Da would awaken, lucid for once. Come looking with his old rifle, find his little girl dancing naked in the storm with a pelt over her shoulders, and...

"Why have you stopped?" The seal girl asked, sliding up warm and soft to Mairead's side at the cliff's edge.

The pelt the girl had found, dusty and forgotten in her father's wardrobe. The way Mansie had mistaken the seal girl for his own wife until Mairead had come in and reminded him of years gone by, and a white stone cross down the Ramphollow churchyard. The frenzy on his face when he'd seen her with the gray skin in her hands. You give it back to me! His fevered digging in the pantry cellar. Mairead's fingers curled tight into the silvery fur at her sides.

The seal girl gasped and shivered against her. "Mairead, what is it? What's wrong?"

"The tide." She managed a nod to the now-flooded trink. "We're trapped. The storm's nearly here."

"We aren't," the girl replied, and slipped her hand, warm and soft, between the sodden hide and Mairead's shoulders. "Surely you know we've another way back."

And she did know. Like any Orkney girl Mairead had spent half her life in the water or on it, and could swim or dive in almost any conditions. But still her heart banged at her throat, so loud she could hardly draw breath to whisper, "I don't know how."

Gently, inexorably, the seal girl turned Mairead's face away from the looming storm, met her stare with solemn, heartbreaking welcome and a tiny, sad smile. "Mairead, beloved of the sea," she said, and smoothed back her hair, "I'm your Umadh. I'll show you the way of it."

"Umadh..." Even the sound of her name was like a kiss, warm and low, sweet as milk and beautiful as butter. It was the most natural thing in the world to let the sound of it pull her down to the kiss itself, to the press of lip, the slide of tongue, the snag of tooth. To yield to clasping hands and pillowing arms, and with a relief so strong it nearly broke her heart, to simply let herself fall.

Not even the whelming sea broke that kiss apart.

The most shocking thing was to find that the dark water was not cold at all. Another time, Mairead might have reasoned that she'd become accustomed to the chill, between the freshening dawn wind, the spray of the turning tide, and the wet pelt over her shoulders. Now, however, such logic failed utterly. The more so as Umadh twisted free of her embrace, rolled about her in a sudden flicker, and caught her beneath the armpits from above, steering them both free of the currents that tugged them toward the rocky holm's root. It took Mairead all of three heartbeats to catch the rhythm of it, and to match Umadh's kicks with her own, so seamlessly that, though the swirl of water tugged at their ankles as they passed, their feet neither knocked nor tangled.

The only dissonance arose when, far later than she'd expected, the urge to breathe came upon Mairead. She shuddered with the effort of choking down the sudden, desperate instinct; tried to twist free of Umadh's grip, and to kick for the surface all at once, yelping out a mouthful of bubbles as her foot scraped hard against the rocky bottom. Something caught her ankle in the dark water—a scrap of weed, a ragged anchor line long forgot, a wicked and hungry Trow, the groping hand of Death himself—and another raft of bubbles burst from her.

Then Umadh was before her, hair like spilled ink in the water, eyes wide and worried, hands tangling in Mairead's hair as she yanked the gray pelt up over her head like the hood of a mac—and suddenly the fear was gone. Mairead's eyes softened to the gloom, picked out a tangle of oakum and wicker, driftwood, weed and netting half caught on the bottom. A tiny kick in the right direction pulled her free of it, and then a fierce wriggle carried her like a bullet to the air.

The last scrap of breath burst from her lips in a spray of seawater and a shout of laughter. The air flooding her lungs was icy and thick with whipping mist, and Mairead drank it down in helpless, giggling gasps as the sea tossed her about like a float cut loose of its net. Umadh erupted from the sea a little way off, the brown pelt's mask draped rakishly over one eye as she took in Mairead's hysteria, and cocked a quizzical eyebrow.

"I'm a seal," Mairead managed at last, her voice breaking over the obvious truth of it, so that she had to say it again, louder. "I'm a seal!" A shout this time, face tipped stormward, so that God, if he was listening above the screeching wind and rowling thunder, would know she'd finally understood.

Umadh swam close, all dark eye and white skin over a ferocious grin. "Is that so?" she asked, arch and beautiful. "A seal should better manage her breathing, don't you think?"

Somehow the slight failed to prick Mairead as it would have done had anyone—islander or ferrylouper—offered it ashore. Perhaps it was the daring, hopeful look in Umadh's eyes, or the memory of just how soft those lips of hers were, how they yielded when pressed, but even in surrender they commanded her to keep up, to follow, to learn. Mairead chuckled, and slapped a sheet of water at her. "All right then Bootless, suppose you show me the way of it, eh?"

Umadh's only response was a daring look, and a sudden dive. Mairead took a lungful, caught the gray pelt's leathery nose like the brim of a cap, and prepared to follow her down, but a sudden, fierce grip on her knee startled that thought clear away. For a second, between kick and thrash, a cloud of floating hair whispered against Mairead's belly, and a welling brush of thick fur slid along the arch of her calf—just reassurance enough to stop her panicked first reaction. It was Umadh's hand on her; Umadh's nose nudging her leg to the side, spreading her to the water; Umadh's shoulders pressing up under her thighs, so that long, dark hair streaked like teasing fingers around Mairead's arse, where Umadh's steadying fingers soon followed.

She's going to... She's... Mairead had no word for it, only longing fantasies conjured from the pages of her brothers' magazines. It was enough to still her breath in her throat, and to tighten her sex in a sudden, whelming clutch of want. The moment stretched thin, driven higher each time the restless sea rolled Mairead backward, only to have Umadh tug her low again, grip bruising-tight, one finger just grazing the furl of her arse. But no touch descended upon her sex, however much Mairead yearned.

"Please," she gulped, mouth just above the blowing foam as the storm rolled in overhead, "Just... please!"

A stream of bubbles rolled up along her sex. Mairead felt her flesh seize at the delicate, maddening touch; heard herself wail through the wind's roar; realized only after her hands filled up with thick, dark hair, that she'd stopped paddling to keep her face above the waves. That Umadh's dead-weight embrace was about to pull her under. Mairead had time for one shallow breath before Umadh's mouth and the stormy waves overcame her.

Taut-strung as she was, Mairead hadn't far at all to go. She'd barely time to fathom the heat and friction, the rough of tongue, the smooth of lip, the restive flickering pressure that gave way to suction, and dear Heaven, those were teeth? There was no naming the sensations, so far and away beyond her own furtive, half-shamed touches on land. Mairead could only hang on, heels wrapping the brown pelt tight around Umadh's wiry shoulders, hands thick in her hair, curved to the fine bones of her skull, not to compel, but just so that she would not float away.

Mairead's lungs ached for the air she could feel, restless with foam just above the crown of her head, but her sex hungered the fiercer, and Umadh, wicked creature, would not let herself be rushed. As though she could feel what her every lick and suckle did to Mairead, as if she could read the tension coiling up spring inside her, each flick of tongue cocking it tighter, but not quite, never quite too much.

Soon Mairead thought she must spend, breathe, or else explode.

In that moment, Umadh's tongue pressed down, flat, hard, merciless—a thumb pressing out a gnat. Mairead found herself thrashing, pulsing, her sex pushing back against that tongue as though to buck it clear, even as her hands clutched Umadh's head close. She screamed a lungful of perfect, glassy spheres into the churning sea, held nothing, not so much as a whisper back, and watched them race away to the surface, careless and silver and perfect... and gone.

She did not, even for an instant, consider letting go.

Umadh carried her, choking, retching, and laughing, to the surface, held her close while the restive waves rolled past beneath them. "Not quite how it's best done, my love," she laughed, slapping Mairead across the shoulders as she coughed up seawater.

Mairead managed half a smile and the ghost of a chuckle. The pink flush across the selkie's face and breasts gave lie to her offhand teasing, and the sweep of speckled velvet gray over Mairead's own shoulder clung, warm, musky, and lush in the blowing sea. It might as well have been a sweaty, gasping embrace within a tangle of skin-hot linen. "Practice," she managed after a few more coughs, "need more practice. I'll get better..."

Umadh laughed, whipping the brown pelt off her shoulders in a silken wriggle, and handing it over to Mairead as the waves bobbed them aloft once more. "We'll come back to this lesson, I think. Let's just move on for now, eh?"

Realizing what must come next, Mairead felt the glow in her belly subside just a bit, felt it roll up tighter, smaller, and tuck itself under something that felt a little like fear. She gave herself no time with it, whipped the gray pelt over her head, gasping just a bit as the water's chill locked around her, only to fade as she pulled the brown pelt—her mother's pelt—over her head in its place.

It settled around her like warm arms and a low voice just made for lullabies, and in its embrace Mairead's fear sulked a bit away.

Not gone, no, but yielding enough that eagerness could again take hold. Here was the magic Mairead had longed for, watched for from frigid heights when the moon lit the holm with welcome, dreamt of when the goodly folk of Ramphollow reminded her again and again, that although she was island born and raised, she just wasn't quite like.

Here was the missing piece. Or rather, here was the place where finally the extra piece, herself, would fit. If somehow the skin her mother had been born in might do for her. Umadh caught her eye as she settled the freckled gray skin around her, and reading something there, offered a smile at once ferocious, triumphant, and dazzling.

"This is the easiest way," she said, pulling the pelt up over her head, but farther this time, so that the empty mask with its whiskers bristling, drooped almost to her chin. "Just pull it close, take a deep breath, and..." she caught the black leather nose in two fingers, pressed it down to her own, "Dive." And like a silver fish, she did.

A moment later, a freckled gray harbor seal spiraled up around Mairead in the water, slick and warm along her leg and hip. It breached with a mocking cackle, and slashed water into her face before rolling off to slice through the waves. A dare if ever there was one. Mairead grinned to herself, hugged her mother's skin close, and gave herself over to the waves with as much of her heart as she could spare.

Equal parts race, tag, keep away, and blatant seduction it was. Mairead the larger, and more powerful, nearly caught Umadh several times, but Umadh was nimbler, cannier, and knew very well just what her sleek, dense body could be made to do in the weightless, churning waves. Each time Mairead nipped at a flipper or flank only to close her teeth on empty brine, or foam, she just knew she was being led precisely where her lover wished her to go. That not a flip or a dive or a mocking splash was anything but meticulously planned, and plotted to show her the way of things.

When Umadh declared an end to the race by flalloping herself effortlessly up onto the end of the jetty, Mairead was certain of it. It took her several tries to work out how to thrust her body out of the water, but when she managed it and humped her way across the rocks, Umadh rewarded her with a cuddle: flank to panting flank, warm together under the driving sky as dawn brought the storm ashore at last.

Mairead felt the rain as the heavens at last opened, knew it was bucketing rough, but found herself amazed at how little it troubled her. A brisk wind, she might have thought it, she ashore and in shoes. Only her face and her flippers felt the sting of the driving rain in any real measure. That was, however, measure enough when it flew full into her eyes.

Mairead reluctantly rolled to turn her face away from the slanting rain. Only then did she spy the boat, cheerily blue as other skies and tucked hastily into the *Ursilla Meur*'s shadow. Only two hasty lines secured her to the cleats, and in the storm, she rattled against the jetty like a drum, adding another layer of noise between the wind's howl and the thunder.

"Aunt Jenn!" Mairead cried, hearing the yelping bark fall from her lips before she remembered herself. The skin pulled loose around her mouth, and as she pushed herself up higher to try and see up the rise to the house, Mairead became aware of the dock, rough under her hands, of the fur slipping away from her legs and face, revealing her to the storm. The dock shuddered under her, and Mairead whirled to find Umadh, still in her fur, charging down the boards, wolfish teeth bared in a snarl, melting eyes gone hard. She scrambled backward, slipped on her fur, and finally tumbled over the edge and back into the sea.

Umadh followed her down in a silvery plunge, caught Mairead's unattached pelt in her jaws as she struggled to pull it around her in the icy water, and lunged away. Mairead managed to keep both her grip and her breath as the powerful harbor seal towed them both out around the point of the jetty, instinct warning her that to lose either would mean death this time. Just as her vision was narrowing, the tugging and the ghostly sensation of teeth clamped upon her shoulder released. Mairead clutched her pelt, her lifeline close, and rocketed up to the air.

"That was the *Fisher King!*" she yelped, almost as soon as her head broke the surface, "And Ben Skerrien's car up by the house as well!" Her throat wound tight to remember—dim forms crowding the white walls, hunched in broad hats and slickers, lanterns pricking the storm-gloom as they carried a narrow shape between them into the house.

"Aye, and you in your fur, calling them down upon us!" Umadh said behind her, voice angry and cold. "Witless ninny, did you mean them to have us both?"

"That's my Da they've come for! With a stretcher!" She kicked herself up as a wave came in, but glimpsed only the house's upper windows, each glowing balefully alight. "You told me he was sleeping!"

"And sleep he does," Umadh bit back, "Just as you knew he must. Death hung close on him the first night I came to you. I know you must have smelled it on him!"

"No, he was fine! He was strong at the wedding, and he... he saved me from..." she couldn't say it, remembering that awful, waiting stillness after Helzie had dragged himself from the house. She had known, even then. Why else had she never insisted upon seeing her father? She'd known, and she despised herself for it now.

"Yes. Even an old, mad thief will still fight to defend his hoard when a young one comes to take it."

Mairead thrashed around in the water. "His hoard? Is that what you think I was to him? He loved me! And he loved my mother as well!"

"Loved her enough to take her for a slave," Umadh hissed back. "Loved her enough to chain her to the land, to bed her and breed her until she died of it. But never loved her enough to set her free. Nor to tell her pups what their blood concealed, neither!" She spat into the water as if she'd have liked a face better.

"You're wrong! She loved him. Aunt Jenn... everyone says she loved him!"

Umadh's glower softened a little with pity. "Mairead, what other choice had she? 'Only so many tears you can swallow before you drown.' That's what the old cows say of it." She swam closer, lay a hand on her shoulder, and kept a stubborn grip when Mairead tried to shrug it off. "Her pups were born in skin, not in fur. How could she leave you, even if he had given her back her freedom? He needn't have kept her skin from her at all, for she'd never have left you. But keep it he did. And he's raised you in a cage as well. And now he's dead... well you may mourn him, but I will not."

Another swell raised them high and, squinting through the rain, Mairead once more glimpsed the house, dark figures passing before the upstairs windows. What a crowd there must be in there. More souls than the lighthouse had seen since the wedding feast back when Mansie wed that strange little bridey he'd brought back from "Australia."

She closed her eyes, struggled against a million words she did not want to say. "And Durn Helzie?" she managed at last, and knew from the flinch in Umadh's eyes that she'd struck true. "He didn't just go home when he left the house, did he? They've come looking for him as well, haven't they?"

Umadh boosted her chin, defiant and angry. "I found that one at the tideline when I hauled out that morning, and so if I helped him into it, 'twas only fair. He meant to steal me from the sea, and so he's gone to feed the sea's children in his turn."

That shocked her enough to wriggle loose, but Umadh, reading the horror in her eyes, only barked one angry laugh. "I don't eat carrion, Mairead! Nor would I eat such reeking trash as that even if I caught him in the tide and swimming, neither. It's lobster bait he was, and so it's to them I left him." She was insulted. Moreover, she was hurt. Mairead guessed if she hadn't needed her arms for treading water, Umadh would have had them crossed tightly over her breasts.

"Lobster bait," she sighed, and lay back against the rolling water so that the rain stung her face and breasts. She could feel the wave take her up, as the others had passed her by, and boost her back toward the tumbled stones of the jetty's end, and the tall, flashing white tower looming above them on the hill.

"Mairead, wait," Umadh called, surging after her to catch her shoulder again. "They mustn't see you, truly!"

"The current along this beach rolls up to the inlet, Umadh," she said, catching a fistful of the gray pelt and using it to pull the girl close. "You know it does. Each time the tide comes in, it sweeps everything on this side of the headland right up past the holm, and all the way inland to the hatchery." She gave Umadh a shake that knocked their knees together under the water. "Did they pull Helzie out of the nets last night with a belly full of shot? Or did he wash up at shipyards instead?"

"I've no—" she bit off the words in a yelp as Mairead shook her by the scruff.

"It's me they're really looking for," she said, pointing at the tower, and the prickle of lanterns and electric torches swinging along the path to the shingle. "They knew we'd fought, Durn and me. They knew I'd walloped him. Good God, I even said I'd shoot him if he came here again. They'll be thinking it was me that killed him!"

For a long moment, they stared, breath steaming together as the rain drove around them. Umadh's dark eyes were so fierce and bright Mairead wondered if she might not lunge and snap like a cornered dog. But instead, she broke the gaze and turned to prize Mairead's hand off her pelt with powerful, icy fingers. "They will, most like," she said, all contrived indifference. "I've noticed land folk have little sense as such things go. But you and I know you did no such thing. Now come away before they reach the shingle. We don't want to be seen like this."

"You... you've taken my life from me! I can never go back again!"

"I never have," Umadh cried, dark eyes blazing as the rain streaked her face. "You're free to go back to the dirt if you will not have me! They'll work out it was the old thief who shot, not you. They'll sniff out the young thief's blood on the shingle. So swim back to the land in your sealskin cloak and tell them you're blameless!" she choked, dashed at her eyes, and pointed back at the searching figures. "Watch how these friends and neighbors of yours fight each other to take that pelt away from you, girlin! They'll prison you in that fine white skin of yours, shackle you to a man you don't want, give you pups just as crippled as yourself, and take away your every chance to get back to the sea."

"You will have to think of a future for yourself soon, Mairead..."

"And old Mansie not yet in his grave, let alone that girl of his married off or moved out of the place..."

"Here now, what's wrong, sunbeam? You get a cramp?"

"Oh, Mairead would much rather dance with me, boys, I'm better her type, you know!"

"Oh, and I'll tell you what all Ramphollow knows, you unnatural creature—"

"It's just a few dances, Mairey, not an engagement..."

"He knows there's some of His children who have no other place to fit into it than underneath His wing..."

Mairead swallowed, clutched at the fur across her shoulders, and tried to imagine again that it was her mother's arms. "And if I go with you?"

"I will love you," Umadh said, voice clogged and low. "I will never force your going, nor your staying, beloved, but I would hunt the waves with you, share with you my shoals and my stones with you. And when the moon came into clear skies, we would dance together with the others, and with ourselves alone." She slipped closer in the water, as though she wished to reach for Mairead, but didn't quite dare anymore. Instead, she whispered, "If you come away with me, I will teach you to love the Sea as her daughter, her treasure, her rightful heir. I will teach you to be free."

Lightning rattled the clouds, still aloft, but Mairead's weather sense could tell it would be tickling the lighthouse tower any minute. Then the searchers would have to abandon the ridgeline and the unsheltered beach until the storm cleared. Not even Skerrien would risk folk in a hellyiefer like this one.

"One spared to the sea is three spared to the land," she heard herself say.

"Aye. We tell that story too," Umadh answered as, in the middle distance, boots echoed along the wooden stretch of the jetty. Only one lantern swung over the boards, and Mairead found she didn't want to guess who might be holding it. Even if it were Aunt Jenn on the jetty, what would she say to her? What could she say anymore?

"Come home, *Ursilla's* daughter; my lovely Mairead," Umadh whispered in her ear, pressed soft against her side for just long enough to leave heat behind when she swam clear again. "Let the land have your brothers," she said, and pulled the gray seal mask down over her face, "I want only you." And then she dove, a flash of silver fur and black leather.

Mairead gasped three breaths—shallow, harsh—struggled to fit them in beside the enormous weight that gathered like a fist in her breast. Then the clouds reached down in violet fire, tickled the lighthouse tower for just a second, and bashed the world flat under the thundercrack. In the woolen silence that followed, Mairead found her lungs full of air, and her mind entirely made up.

"This is the God that made you," she said Father Brian's words to herself, just for the muted feel of them on her lips. "Can you really think He doesn't understand what you feel?"

Then Mairead put the land and its flashing white tower to her back, pulled her mother's pelt close around her, and commended her body at last to the waves.

About the Author

Catt Kingsgrave has been writing fiction and verse since the early eighties, and despite everything, has not yet seen fit to desist. With works ranging from Urban and Mythic Fantasy through Horror, Erotica, and a decided taste for the Gothic and macabre, she takes delight in making all her works as difficult to classify as humanly possible. She lives with her partner, five cats, and two snakes in an upstate New York home that was built a century or so before the state in which she was born was made a part of the Union. When not writing, she has been known to indulge in random bouts of theater, songwriting, dance, painting, home repair, volunteer rape crisis counseling, and folk music. Her interests are zombie outbreak preparedness, criminal profiling, gardening, and full-contact applied mythology. She does not make jam.

other titles you may enjoy from Circlet Press!

Like a Queen: Lesbian Erotic Fairy Tales
edited by Cecilia Tan & Rachel Kincaid
$5.99   ISBN: 978-1-885865-83-0

Five lesbian fairytales that feature classic stories with a queer twist. What are the erotic possibilities of the enchanted princesses and forbidding queens that we learned about as children? Instead of competing for princes or beauty, the women in these stories are made more powerful by their desire for each other.

Women On The Edge of Space
edited byDanielle Bodnar & Cecilia Tan
$3.99   ISBN: 978-1-61390-019-2

In these four stories, women explore the uncharted trails of human desire as they rocket through space and transcend time and place. They inspire fear and hope in the face of danger and uncertainty, and the thrills of satiating a hunger for intimacy in a strange new world.

Like a Coming Wave: Oceanic Erotica
edited by Andrea Trask
$5.99   ISBN: 978-1-61390-041-3

The ocean is a vast playground of creatures real and imagined, rife with power and depth. In these eight stories fantasy's best writers explore the erotic potential in the world of water. Mermaids and -men, selkies, Greek gods, and even kraken cavort in these pages.